THE FACTORY ON
THE CLIFF

The following titles are all in the *Fonthill Complete A. G. Macdonell* Series.
The year indicates when the first edition was published.
See **www.fonthillmedia.com** for details.

Fiction

England, their England   (1933)
How Like an Angel   (1934)
Lords and Masters   (1936)
The Autobiography of a Cad   (1939)
Flight From a Lady   (1939)
Crew of the Anaconda   (1940)

Short Stories

The Spanish Pistol   (1939)

Non-Fiction

Napoleon and his Marshals   (1934)
A Visit to America   (1935)
My Scotland   (1937)

Crime and Thrillers written under the pseudonym of John Cameron

The Seven Stabs   (1929)
Body Found Stabbed   (1932)

Crime and Thrillers written under the pseudonym of Neil Gordon

The New Gun Runners   (1928)
The Factory on the Cliff   (1928)
The Professor's Poison   (1928)
The Silent Murders   (1929)
The Big Ben Alibi   (1930)
Murder in Earl's Court   (1931)
The Shakespeare Murders   (1933)

THE FACTORY ON THE CLIFF

A. G. MACDONELL

Originally published under the pseudonym of
NEIL GORDON

FONTHILL

Fonthill Media Limited
www.fonthillmedia.com
office@fonthillmedia.com

First published 1928
This edition published in the United Kingdom 2012

British Library Cataloguing in Publication Data:
A catalogue record for this book is available from the British Library

Copyright © in Introduction, Fonthill Media 2012

ISBN: 978-1-78155-024-3 (print)
ISBN: 978-1-78155-170-7 (e-book)

Typeset in 11pt on 14pt Sabon.
Printed and bound in England.

Contents

Introduction to the 2012 Edition 7

I   The Golfing Holiday 11

II   The Plans Made in the Smoking Room 15

III   The Mysterious Irishman 25

IV   The Girl from the Factory on the Cliff 31

V   Sir Alastair Chisholm 42

VI   The Inquisitive Mr Templeton 49

VII   The Four Allies head for London 58

VIII   Inspector Roberts of Scotland Yard 66

IX   The Mysterious Mr Morton 70

X   Sir Alastair Sails to Madeira 78

XI   The Meeting with Susan Blake 83

XII   The Warehouse in the East End 91

XIII   The Deadly Discovery 99

XIV   Woodridge 115

XV   By Hispano-Suiza to Scotland 124

XVI   Sea-borne Visitors to the Factory 135

XVII   The Attack 141

XVIII   The Arrival of the Navy 148

XIX   The Organizer of Liberty 155

Introduction
to the 2012 Edition

As a satirist, A. G. Macdonell achieved fame and critical recognition, but it was as a crime and thriller writer in his early literary career that his prodigious abilities in character depiction and observation took root. Many of his most memorable characters, devious plots and witty observations are exhibited in these early works, and *Factory on the Cliff*, first published in 1928, is no exception. It is one of several crime and thriller novels written by Macdonell under the pseudonym Neil Gordon.

Archibald Gordon Macdonell — Archie — was born on 3 November 1895 in Poona, India, the younger son of William Robert Macdonell of Mortlach, a prominent merchant in Bombay, and Alice Elizabeth, daughter of John Forbes White, classical scholar and patron of the arts. It seems likely that Archie was named after Brevet-Colonel A. G. Macdonell, CB, presumably an uncle, who commanded a force that defeated Sultan Muhammed Khan at the fort of Shabkader in the Afghan campaign of 1897.

The family left India in 1896 and Archie was brought up at 'Colcot' in Enfield, Middlesex, and the Macdonell family home of 'Bridgefield', Bridge of Don, Aberdeen. He was educated at Horris Hill preparatory school near Newbury, and Winchester College, where he won a scholarship. Archie left school in 1914, and two years later, he joined the Royal Field Artillery of the 51st Highland Division as a second lieutenant. His experiences fighting on the Western Front were to have a great influence on the rest of his life.

The 51st, known by the Germans as the 'Ladies from Hell' on account of their kilts, were a renowned force, boasting engagements at Beaumont-Hamel, Arras, and Cambrai. But by the time of the 1918 Spring Offensives, the division was war-worn and under strength; it suffered heavily and Archie Macdonell was invalided back to England, diagnosed with shell shock.

After the war, Macdonell worked with the Friends' Emergency and War Victims Relief Committee, a Quaker mission, on reconstruction in eastern Poland and famine in Russia. Between 1922 and 1927 he was on the headquarters staff of the League of Nations Union, which has prominent mention in *Flight from a Lady* (1939) and *Lords and Masters* (1936). In the meantime he stood unsuccessfully as Liberal candidate for Lincoln in the general elections of 1923 and '24. On 31 August 1926, Macdonell married Mona Sabine Mann, daughter of the artist Harrington Mann and his wife, Florence Sabine Pasley. They had one daughter, Jennifer. It wasn't a happy marriage and they divorced in 1937, Mona citing her husband's adultery.

A. G. Macdonell began his career as an author in 1927 writing detective stories, sometimes under the pseudonyms Neil Gordon or John Cameron. He was also highly regarded at this time as a pugnacious and perceptive drama critic; he frequently contributed to the *London Mercury*, a literary journal founded in 1919 by John Collings Squire, the poet, writer, and journalist, and Archie's close friend.

By 1933 Macdonell had produced nine books, but it was only with the publication in that year of *England, Their England* that he truly established his reputation as an author. A gentle, affectionate satire of eccentric English customs and society, *England, Their England* was highly praised and won the prestigious James Tait Black Award in 1933. Macdonell capitalized on this success with another satire, *How Like an Angel* (1934), which parodied the 'bright young things' and the British legal system. The military history *Napoleon and his Marshals* (1934) signalled a new direction; although Macdonell thought it poorly rewarded financially, the book was admired by military experts, and it illustrated the range of his abilities. Between 1933 and 1941, A. G. Macdonell produced eleven more books, including the superlative *Lords and Masters* (1936), which tore into 1930s upper-class hypocrisy in a gripping and prescient thriller, and *The Autobiography of a Cad* (1939), an hilarious mock-memoir of one Edward Fox-Ingleby, ruthless landowner, unscrupulous politician, and consummate scoundrel.

In 1940 Macdonell married his second wife, Rose Paul-Schiff, a Viennese whose family was connected with the banking firm of Warburg Schiff. His health had been weak since the First World War, and he died suddenly of heart failure in his Oxford home on 16 January 1941, at the age of 45.

A tall, athletic man with a close-cropped moustache, he was remembered as a complex individual, 'delightful ... but quarrelsome and choleric' by the writer Alec Waugh, who called him the Purple Scot, and by J. B. Morton, as 'a man of conviction, with a quick wit and enthusiasm and ... a sense of compassion for every kind of unhappiness.'

Factory on the Cliff, one of Macdonell's early thrillers, is a fast-paced, Buchanesque adventure of international espionage, a reluctant hero, and a deadly poison that threatens to wipe out the western world. It is a wonderful example of Macdonell's precious ability to transfer his own unmistakable enjoyment in writing directly onto the reader.

CHAPTER I

The Golfing Holiday

George Templeton's car refused to start on the self-starter. He jumped out impatiently and gave the handle a mighty twist. The engine back-fired and dislocated his thumb and he found himself unable to play golf for the remainder of his holiday.

He had taken rooms in a small hotel in the North-East of Scotland, intending to play golf twice or even three times a day throughout the three weeks of his leave. The accident happened at the end of the first week, and left him in a very bad temper, with a fortnight to spend as best he could. Like so many men who are prepared to walk seven or ten miles so long as they are hitting a golf ball, Templeton intensely disliked walking even one mile along a country road. However, there was no other available exercise, and he therefore set out every morning for a daily plod of several miles in order to pass the time.

On the third morning after the unfortunate back-fire, Templeton chanced to stroll northwards along the sea-coast, a part of the country which he had hitherto not explored. He was in a sulky frame of mind as he reflected on the wonderful golf which he might have been playing at that moment, and on the callous cheerfulness of his friends in the hotel who had set off for the first tee as he was finishing his breakfast.

It was a beautiful, sunny morning, but the good weather only annoyed him. If it had been pouring with rain, things would not have been so bad, but it was just like his luck that the weather should improve as soon as he was out of action. He was, in fact, in a nasty temper.

He had gone some three or four miles along the lonely stretch of rocky coast when he was aroused from his meditations by the approach of a large motor-lorry which almost blocked the entire width of the narrow country road, so that Templeton had to shrink back against the stone wall in order to avoid being hit. This only served to increase his annoyance, and he pursued his walk, grumbling about the inconsiderateness of motor-drivers and cursing in general the men who had invented motor-cars.

A little further on, he came to the top of a long, gradual hill, and could see the road sloping away to the north for a considerable distance. He sat down and began to fill a pipe when the same lorry came back up the hill and clattered past him at a much faster rate than it had previously been going. Templeton growled at it as it went past but the driver paid no attention and Templeton had a glimpse of a man who looked distinctly frightened; the next minute it had disappeared out of sight in the direction from which it had originally come.

When the pipe was lit, George Templeton proceeded at a leisurely pace. On reaching the bend at the foot of the hill, he saw, a few hundred yards away, three or four men walking slowly towards him and obviously searching for something in the long grass at each side of the road. The lorry was standing a little distance beyond them. As the searchers came nearer, he saw to his surprise that he knew one of them by sight. It was one Griffin, who had been at Cambridge with him. Although he had been merely a bowing acquaintance in undergraduate days nevertheless he stepped up to him and said cordially, "Hullo, Griffin! Whoever would have thought of seeing you here?"

The other started and replied, "My name is not Griffin and I don't know who you are." Templeton looked at him for a second, and then said stiffly, "I beg your pardon. A stupid mistake."

The other pushed past him and resumed his search.

Templeton was puzzled, as he knew perfectly well that the man was Griffin, and he was fairly certain that Griffin had recognized him. He decided not to be put off by rudeness.

"Lost something, I observe," he said, more in order to annoy the other man than to prolong the conversation. "Can I help you?"

Griffin paid no attention, and at last one of the other men looked up and said, "No, thanks," and accompanied his words with such a scowl that Templeton began to feel amused.

"Do tell me what you are looking for," he went on. "I have spent so many years of my life looking for golf balls that I am quite certain I could help you."

None of the four replied and Templeton's spirits began to rise. He ostentatiously took up a position behind the searchers and began to poke in the grass with his stick. The man who had refused his offer of help turned and said, "What are you doing there? We don't want your help."

"Nor do I want yours," said Templeton blandly. "This is a public road and I am looking for a collar-stud which I dropped here last Tuesday week."

The man who had denied that his name was Griffin interposed sharply and said, "Come on, Tom! Don't hang about here"; and without another word the party made their way up the hill, with bent backs and slow steps. Templeton followed them for a minute or two and then, quickening his steps, he passed the searchers and began to search on his own in front of them.

In less than a minute he had found what they were looking for. Templeton, who had been an infantry officer in the war, instantly recognized that the small dark object lying in a thick bed of nettles was first cousin to a Mills bomb. The pattern was different and the shape different, but the pin was there and it was obviously the same kind of weapon.

"Here you are, Griffin!" he shouted. "What prize do I get for finding the thimble?"

He took up the bomb and was surprised to find how light it was. The four men ran forward and Griffin made a snatch at it.

"Manners, manners," said Templeton reprovingly. "On trust, there's a good dog. When I say 'Paid for,' out comes the pin and you get the dough-nut." He made a motion as if to pull out the pin. The other started back and his face went white. "Good God, man," he exclaimed. "Don't do that. It'll go off."

Templeton started. "Is it charged?" he asked.

"Yes," said Griffin.

"Then it's yours," was the prompt reply. "Free, gratis and for nothing."

Griffin seized it eagerly from him, and then the four men turned without a word of thanks and ran down the hill and round the corner.

"Well, I'm blowed," said Templeton aloud. "There's manners for you," and he sat down on the dyke and watched the proceedings.

In a short time the lorry once more appeared and began to climb the hill. The driver was alone on the front seat and there was no room for anyone to sit among the closely packed wooden boxes which formed the cargo. Templeton, therefore, assumed that the three others were still on the road or near it, and he set off at a swinging pace down the hill in pursuit. On rounding the corner, he saw no sign of his quarry and he concluded that they had taken a side road which led down towards the cliffs.

At first he thought that the cart-track, for it was little more, was simply a path used by fishermen going down to their nets, when his eye happened to notice that it emerged again from under cover of the rocks some little distance up the coast, and appeared to end at a cluster of buildings situated almost on the edge of the cliffs.

As he stood speculating on the nature of these buildings and wondering what sort of person chose to live in a place so exposed to all the winds of heaven, he saw a large motor-car moving slowly from the cluster of buildings along the cart track. He watched while it disappeared below the level of the cliffs and emerged again to join the road on which he was Standing. As it passed him, he saw that the only occupant besides the driver was a man of exceptionally swarthy complexion. He was quite clearly not a citizen of the British Isles, and Templeton judged that he must be an Arab or something akin to an Arab. The car rapidly accelerated when it reached the better road, and vanished over the top of the hill.

Greatly puzzled by the curious happenings of the morning, Templeton retraced his steps to the hotel and arrived just in time to see the golfers trooping back from their morning round. At lunch he was compelled to listen to innumerable stories of how one had holed a long putt at the crucial moment, and how another would have won if it had not been for some unparalleled stroke of misfortune.

CHAPTER II

The Plans Made in the Smoking Room

That evening in the small smoking-room of the Links Hotel, Templeton related the happenings of the morning to one of his golfing acquaintances who had also been up at Cambridge at the same period. His name was Snell, and he remembered Griffin distinctly. "He was a brilliant fellow," he said, "so far as I can remember. Tall, with a pale face and spectacles, always running about with big books under his arm. He had a beastly sarcastic grin and a sharp tongue."

"That's the man," said Templeton. "I didn't know him much myself,"

"Nobody ever did," said Snell. "It was the same when he went into the Army."

"Do you mean to say that creature was a soldier?" said Templeton in surprise.

"Well, not exactly a soldier," said the other. "He did something with gas at G.H.Q.; either that or making skins for airships. I don't remember which it was, but it was something confoundedly technical. He came a cropper, though, towards the end of the war. I don't know what happened, but someone told me that the Armistice came in the nick of time and they demobilized him instead of firing him out."

The conversation was interrupted by the entrance of a stranger, a tall, very broad-shouldered man with a dark, gloomy face, who sat down and called for a whisky and water. His voice instantly proclaimed him an Irishman.

Templeton said "Good evening" to him, and added that it had been a fine day; but the new-comer was disinclined for conversation and after finishing his drink, he retired from the room.

"Not a very sociable bird," said Snell. "Well, what about Griffin? Shall we run out and have a look at the place before dinner?"

"Let's find out first if the landlord knows anything about it," said Templeton.

In a few minutes they had learned all that the proprietor of the hotel knew about the little colony of strangers who had settled down on the coast shortly after the war. They were scientists engaged on some intricate inquiry into the movements of fishes. No one, so far as the landlord knew, had ever been inside their laboratories, or, indeed, into the house itself, but it was generally believed that they had an enormous tank below the level of the cliffs in which they put the fish which they caught. The idea was that they marked the fish in some way with brass rings or the like and released them on the chance of their being caught again by someone else in some other part of the world. In this way valuable information would be obtained on fish-migration. Whatever was the truth about the tank, at any rate it was true that they had offered a reward of £5 to anyone who would bring back one of the fish which they had marked, and it was rumoured that the skipper of a Grimsby trawler had brought one back and had been given a £5 note for it.

It was all very vague. Even the fortunate skipper from Grimsby had not actually been seen by anyone, so far as the landlord knew. In fact, information about the place, which was generally called the Gulls' Cove or the Gulls' Farm, was very meagre. The strangers had their own housekeeper, and most of their supplies came from London by train. It was obvious that there was a grievance against them for bringing so little custom to the countryside.

"Well, that's that," said Snell, as the landlord left the room. "That is just the sort of thing Griffin would be doing."

"But you don't conduct scientific inquiries into the movements of fishes with the help of a Mills bomb," protested Templeton.

"That's true," said Snell; "but are you sure it was a bomb?"

"If it wasn't, it was the best imitation I've ever seen."

"Well, let's get the car and have a look."

"It will have to be yours," said Templeton. "I'm sick of cars at the moment."

The two acquaintances surveyed the cluster of buildings through field-glasses from the point at which Templeton had seen the swarthy gentleman in the motor-car, but they learned little except that the buildings were encircled by a strong, high, barbed wire fence in which there was only one apparent entrance.

"They are pretty secretive about their fishes," said Snell. "Let's get a bit closer." They drove down the cart-track, halted at the bend where it dipped below the level, and proceeded on foot until they reached a point from which a good view could be obtained. The buildings inhabited by the mysterious scientists consisted of a house, solidly built of Aberdeen granite and roofed with slate, which stood on the edge of the cliff. Behind the house three long barns had been built at some later period. They formed three sides of a square, the farmhouse itself being the fourth side. One peculiarity struck the two observers at once. The barns, which were made of brick, were actually built on to the farm, so that there was no way of getting inside the square except through the farm. For the long low barns had neither door nor window with the exception of an occasional slit, high up from the ground, which added to the fortress-like appearance of the whole cluster of buildings. There was a small side-door in the farm, but the main entrance was obviously in the front, facing the sea. Between the wire entanglement and the barns were the tracks of many motor wheels. In spite of the defensive look of the place nothing could have been more peaceful. A thin curl of smoke was rising slowly from the chimney of the house, and the complete stillness was only broken by the murmur of the waves against the rocks below, and the occasional cry of a gull.

"What's the next move?" said Snell at last. "Do we go and ring the bell and say we have seen a haddock with a gold ring on its tail, or do we wait till midnight and break into the house?"

"What about that bomb?" said Templeton, ignoring the question. "That's the thing that puzzles me; and why did Griffin say he was not Griffin? I suppose we are not doing any good hanging about here anyway. We'll hire a boat tomorrow and have a look at the place from the sea."

"You can do that by yourself," retorted Snell. "I'm going to play golf."

At that moment the small door at the side of the house opened and a girl came out. She walked straight to the gate in the wire entanglement, opened it, and came down the path towards them. She was not dressed as a girl in the country dresses, but as a London girl dresses when she is in the country. She wore neat but strong brogues, stockings of the latest "sports" pattern, a short tweed skirt and a silk jumper. She was small and slight, with blue eyes and fair hair. She would have appeared to be a typical damsel of the "fair and fluffy" school, if her face had not been so white that there was not a vestige of colour in her cheeks, and if her mouth had not been closed tightly, indicating a young lady of considerable character and determination.

The two men stood rather sheepishly while this small vision walked up to them and said without any hesitation, "It's a fine evening." They took their hats off and mumbled something. They were both completely taken by surprise by the girl's direct approach. There was a momentary silence and then she went on, "This is a lovely part of the coast."

Snell was the first to recover his composure, and he said, "It is now." The girl smiled for the fraction of a second and then her lips came together again with almost the snap of a mouse-trap. Templeton turned on his friend and said, "Don't be an ass." The girl narrowed her blue eyes a little and stared calmly first at Snell and then at Templeton. Both young men were slightly embarrassed at the scrutiny. "It is not very kind," she said at last, "to call your friend an ass for making such a handsome speech," and then without another word she turned and walked back to the wire fence, let herself through, and vanished into the house.

The two friends watched her movements in silence, and when she disappeared they turned and simultaneously said to each other: "Well, what do you know about that!" They stared at the house, at the sea, at the rocks, at the wire fence, at the country round and at the sky as if some possible explanation might be found in any one of these places. At last Snell observed in a dreamy tone: "I suppose it's consorting with fish that makes people so eccentric, but she certainly was a remarkably pretty girl. I think I'll come with you tomorrow in the boat after all, Templeton."

"You stick to your golf, Snell, my lad," replied Templeton. "This is no place for you. I am sorry I let you in this. Hallo, here's another motor-car. No, it's the same one," he added, as a limousine came jolting over the cart-ruts. This time the passenger in the back was not the swarthy-faced gentleman, but the big, morose Irishman from the smoking-room in the hotel. He was evidently expected, as a man came out and unlocked the gate to let him in. The limousine jolted round the inside of the wire fence and vanished behind the buildings at the other side.

The two friends retraced their steps to their two-seater and returned to the hotel. A broad-shouldered, muscular youth was standing on the steps of the Links Hotel. He had a red complexion and a cheerful, not particularly intelligent face. He came to meet them. "I've fixed up a four-ball match for the afternoon tomorrow, Harry," he said to Snell.

"Count me out," said Snell. "I'm not playing golf tomorrow."

The newcomer stared incredulously at him, a deep, puzzled frown gradually extinguishing his cheerfulness. He was too taken aback at the unprecedented nature of the crisis to say a word. Snell took advantage of the pause to murmur, "Let me introduce — Mr Templeton — Mr Armstrong." A huge red hand shot out and Templeton had only just time to save his dislocated thumb from being seized in a bear-like grip.

"What's the matter with Harry?" said Mr Armstrong, slowly recovering.

"I'm going out rowing," replied Snell.

"The man's mad," said the muscular youth sadly. "He thinks he's at Shepperton or Sonning in a punt with a lovely charmer."

Snell slipped his arm through that of his friend and said, "Come and have a drink while I tell you about it."

They took him into the smoking-room and rapidly outlined all that had happened. When they had finished the story, Armstrong solemnly rose and said, "Henry Snell, if you are going to abandon two first-class games of golf tomorrow for a cock-and-bull story about bombs and negroes and wire entanglements, you are not the man I took you for. What was the girl like? Was she pretty?"

"I wonder who the Irishman is," said Templeton, pointedly changing the subject. "And what he is doing out there."

"Let's ask the landlord," said Snell; but they learned little from him about their fellow guest. The landlord had never seen him before. He had telegraphed from Belfast reserving a room. "If you ask me," said the man indignantly, "there are too many queer foreigners in these parts. There was a Chinaman up here two or three months ago. I have nothing against him and he paid his bill in good money, and a Chinaman's money is as good as anybody else's, but all the same I don't like having yellow people about, nor black ones either. It puts people against a house."

"Do you get many black ones?" put in Templeton quickly.

"I have not had one now for nearly a year," said the landlord. "But I had two about this time last year, and then there was a Spanish sort of gentleman, Italian or Portuguese or what not. I don't know exactly what he was, but he came up for a day or two. I like English visitors up here, and not any of these fancy foreigners. None of the others stayed very long either. It's not as if they took a room for a month or two; just a couple of days and then away again. It is something to do with these fishes, I expect. It isn't good for business, gentlemen, as you can readily understand."

After dinner Templeton discussed with Snell the events of the day all over again from the beginning, while Armstrong slept on a sofa, and they finally agreed that there was nothing in the least suspicious except the bomb by the roadside. The fact that Griffin had denied his identity was thoroughly in keeping with what they remembered of Griffin's character. They simply put it down to the eccentricity of genius. The barbed wire entanglements and the seclusion of the house could be ascribed to the precautions of scientists on the verge of some great discovery. The behaviour of the girl was dismissed as inexplicable, but no more inexplicable than the behaviour of any other girl. But all three of them admitted that the bomb was difficult to explain.

"It may have been a scientific apparatus," said Templeton, "but it looked too much like the other thing, and you ought to have seen their faces when I pretended that I was going to pull out the pin."

"Well," said Snell finally, "I move that we give up golf tomorrow and all go and have a look at the place from the sea."

"And I," said Armstrong, waking up at that moment, "I oppose the motion. You can do what you like. I'm going to play golf."

With that the three men went to bed.

Next morning Templeton was out early examining the weather. The glass was high and there was every prospect of another sunny, windless day. The landlord of the hotel arranged for the hire of a large, heavy, rowing boat, the type in which the local fishermen examine their nets during the salmon fishing season.

"It is a heavy boat," said the landlord, "but I'm afraid it is the best I can do. Pleasure boats are not very common in these parts."

"That's all right," said Templeton. "I shan't have to row because of my finger, so I don't mind how heavy it is. Snell will grouse, though."

Snell did grouse. He gave one look at the boat and then turned to Templeton. "What's the great idea?" he asked coldly. "Are you going to cox this racing skiff while I scull it along the top of the waves? What do you take me for?"

Templeton grinned. "I was afraid you might make a fuss about it. It isn't really very heavy. You mustn't judge it by its looks."

Snell kicked the boat. "What's its name? The Ocean Greyhound or the Silver Arrow? I'm not going to pull my arms out of their sockets over that hulk."

"All right. You needn't come. I told you before you'd be much better playing golf."

"And leave that lovely fairy to you? Not likely."

"You're not much of a cavalier if you won't take the trouble to row a little boat a few hundred yards to see the girl," said Templeton.

"I don't mind rowing," said Snell. "What I object to is dislocating my arms for the benefit of a rival cavalier who sits quietly and steers."

At that moment Snell's muscular friend, Armstrong, loomed up on the skyline and came rolling down towards them.

"Well, young man," began Snell sternly. "And why aren't you playing golf?" Armstrong laughed. "I couldn't help thinking about you two going off by yourselves. Might have a nasty accident."

"Liar," said his friend calmly. "You were thinking about the Gaiety-chorus peach we saw yesterday." He stopped and stared at his friend and then at the boat and then at his friend again. "A Rugger international and a heavy-weight boxer," he said thoughtfully. "Come on, Bill. You can have a front-row seat in the stalls if you'll do a little rowing. Here's the boat. That sportsman there is the cox because he swears he's hurt his hand. You can stroke and I'll take bow."

Armstrong looked at the boat and said simply, "All right. Have you got anything to eat?"

"Sandwiches and flasks; enough for three."

"Good."

The day turned out as fine as they could possibly have expected and there was only the slightest of breezes. The boat moved a good deal better than Snell had anticipated and by noon they had reached the first of the two rocky headlands which sheltered the Gulls' Cove. They tied up their boat to a boulder and advanced round the headland on foot, creeping cautiously from rock to rock, until they had reached a point from which they could see the whole cove.

The house was silhouetted against the western sky. Immediately in front of it a steep grassy slope fell away to the level of the sea. It would have been possible but very laborious to ascend the slope and therefore a narrow winding path had been made, leading from the front door of the farm down to the small sandy beach at the foot. The two rocky headlands which jutted out into the sea on each side made a perfect shelter and the cove was visible only from the sea and from the farmhouse itself.

A couple of rowing boats were drawn up on the little beach and a small motor-boat lay at anchor. There was as little sign of life as there had been on the land side the previous day. The three men sat down in an angle formed by the rocks and surveyed the whole establishment again with field-glasses.

For at least an hour nothing happened, and Armstrong began to grumble about his lost game of golf. Then at last a little diversion occurred when the motor lorry which Templeton had passed and repassed on the previous day backed out of the end of one of the barns. It stood for a moment and then a man came out on foot and opened a large gate in the wire entanglements. The lorry drove through, made the circuit of the entanglements and disappeared in a southerly direction.

"I can't see any sign of the famous tank," said Snell, "where they teach the kippers to jump through hoops. It looks to me as if all the work is done up above. What about going up the path and having a look?"

"Too dangerous, I should think," said Templeton. "How would you explain what you were doing when you get there? There's the girl again," he added. Armstrong looked up eagerly.

The girl looked out of the door of the house and stood for a moment looking out to sea. The three spies huddled back under cover of the rocks. The girl went into the house and came out the next minute with a pair of field-glasses with which she swept the horizon.

"Looking for fish, I suppose," muttered Snell. At last she put down the glasses and came slowly down the path to the sea.

"We shall look pretty silly if she spots us again," said Templeton. "Can you get round the corner, Armstrong, without being seen?"

Armstrong moved cautiously on hands and knees backwards towards their boat, but he was unfortunately wearing his golfing shoes and the nails slid on a smooth slab of rock, bringing him down with a clatter and a loud exclamation.

In an instant the girl had stopped and was scanning the rocks with her field-glasses. Then she turned towards the house and called out something. Next moment a couple of men came running round the corner of the farm-house and began to descend the path. The three friends, seeing that concealment was useless, tumbled back into their boat with the utmost rapidity and began pulling for home.

"Here's a state of things," said Snell, tugging at the heavy oar. "If they get that motor-boat after us, they will come along and say all kinds of rude things."

They had hardly gone a hundred yards when his fears were realized and the little motor-boat shot out round the corner of the headland.

"Well, we can take it easy," said Snell, resting on his oar, "and prepare to repel boarders." But the motor-boat had apparently no intention of following them. It came to a halt and there was a long pause while both sides surveyed each other through field-glasses. Then the motor-boat turned and slipped back into the little harbour.

"Thank Heaven there were no bombs about," said Snell. "I wished for one moment that I was playing golf. I suggest we get back and not meddle any more in other people's affairs." "I haven't had a chance of seeing the girl," grumbled Armstrong, taking up his oar.

They returned to the inn and found the silent Irishman consuming whisky after whisky in the smoking-room. He was as uncommunicative as before.

Late that evening a note was handed into the hotel addressed to G. Templeton, Esq. Templeton opened it and read as follows:

DEAR SIR,

If you and your two friends will come to the front door of your hotel at 11.15 this evening, you will receive a full explanation of the events which have been puzzling you during the last forty-eight hours.

The note was unsigned and Templeton whistled as he read it. He showed it to Snell and Armstrong; the latter was rather impressed, but Snell shared Templeton's view that it read like an extract from a cheap melodramatic novel. What the purpose of it was, they could not guess. Armstrong took it very seriously. "It's a decoy," he said at last, "to get us out in the open and murder us."

Snell and Templeton laughed. "People don't get murdered in Scotland just for going about in a rowing boat," said Snell. "It's a practical joke of Griffin's."

"Well, anyway," said Templeton, "it's ten minutes past eleven now. I suggest we go out and see what it is."

"Don't be a fool," said Armstrong. "You'll get done in."

Snell patted his large friend affectionately on the back. "You jolly old donkey," he said.

"We need not go beyond the door of the hotel," said Templeton. "Come on! We may be late."

They hustled the reluctant Armstrong down the passage just as the grandfather clock in the hall chimed the quarter. Templeton opened the front door of the hotel cautiously, inch by inch, and peered out. It was a dark night and there were clouds over the stars. Then a voice whispered from the road a few yards distant.

"Is that you, Templeton? It is Griffin speaking. Are your two friends there?"

Templeton kept the door ajar and said, "What do you want with them?"

"I want your help badly," said the voice. "I am in the devil of a hole."

Templeton opened the door wider and the three young men peered out into the darkness. There was a sudden tremendous flash in the road at which they instinctively recoiled back into the passage, but there was no sound.

"What was that?" muttered Snell.

"God knows," said Templeton; and then they heard the footsteps of a man running down the road and receding in the distance.

CHAPTER III

The Mysterious Irishman

The three men waited in the dark passage for a moment or two, and at last Snell said quietly: "I vote we stay indoors for the rest of the evening. There may be more of them waiting for us outside. What do you think it was?"

"A bomb, of course," answered Armstrong, "only it didn't go off."

"A very odd sort of bomb," said Templeton, "to make all that flash and no noise."

"Well, whatever it was," said Armstrong, "I am going to stay indoors. I think we've had a narrow squeak."

Next morning they examined the front of the hotel with the utmost care, but found nothing. There were no marks in the road or on the gravel path which led up to the hotel steps, either of a bomb exploding or failing to explode, or of an effort to remove tracks or traces. They finally dismissed the incident with the verdict that it was typical of Griffin's eccentricity to play an idiotic practical joke that had neither joke nor point.

"All the same," added Templeton, "there are a lot of funny things happening round here."

"Come on and play golf," said Armstrong impatiently to Snell; and the two men departed in the direction of the first tee, leaving Templeton to nurse his dislocated thumb and to occupy himself as best he could in the hotel.

He spent an hour carefully examining the visitors' book and the entries contained in it for the last few years. The names, as might have been expected, were mainly those of holidaymaking golfers like himself, for the hotel was famous in a small circle of Englishmen as a cheap and comfortable inn, near a little-known but first-class golf-course. There were, however, at intervals in the visitors' book, names that were obviously foreign. There were two Chinese names, for instance, and one that might have fitted the Oriental whom he had seen in the limousine car, and the name Alexandrovski appeared no fewer than eight times. Templeton casually asked the landlord about this "Alexandrovski" and found that he was an enthusiastic golfer who visited the hotel solely for the purpose of playing golf. He was hardly ever off the links, according to the landlord. It was a foreign sort of name but the man was English all right. Templeton made a note of the man's address which was in a fashionable square near the centre of London. He also made a complete list of the foreigners' names and addresses which occurred in the book on the off chance that they might have some bearing on the peculiar establishment on the cliffs.

Just before lunch a small motor-car drew up in front of the hotel and two strangers descended. Templeton, who was smoking a pipe by the steps, could not fail to notice the strong Irish accent in which they asked for rooms. They were both small men, with sharp eyes and an alert, determined manner. They appeared to know exactly what they wanted and the best way of getting it.

They sat by themselves at lunch and said not a word; afterwards, one of them retired upstairs while the other pulled an easy chair out to the front door and sat in the sun at the top of the hotel Steps. He remained there, apparently without moving, until about five o'clock, when his companion came downstairs and took his place.

The day was fine and all the other golfers in the hotel were out on the links. The stranger who had been relieved from his post at the front door walked briskly through the public rooms of the hotel until he found George Templeton sitting alone in a corner of the smoking-room. In a few minutes a conversation had begun, of the light, disconnected sort that is common between two strangers in a hotel lounge. Templeton, however, had been so interested and excited by the curious recent incidents that he suspected everyone in the hotel and outside of it being engaged in some mysterious plot. He therefore treated the Irishman's advances with the utmost caution and said as little as possible.

"It's a long way from here to Wicklow," said the little man, to which proposition Templeton cautiously assented.

"You won't get many Irishmen up in these parts," went on the other, but this time Templeton declined to be drawn, and said nothing. "Though, I expect," pursued the other, almost to himself, "you would get a few in the Catholic College in Aberdeen or perhaps they come to Banffshire. There are a lot of Catholics up there, I am told."

Templeton said nothing, and the Irishman eyed him sharply. "It's bad luck you should have come by your accident," he said. It keeps you indoors, I suppose."

"Oh, I go out walking," said Templeton.

"Walking is a great sport for those that like it," said the Irishman. "I hate it."

"So do I"

"You haven't had much of a walk today, for instance," went on the little man. "Is this your normal day's exercise?"

"No, I have been unusually lazy today," admitted Templeton. "As a rule I go for at least an hour in the morning."

There was a pause, and then the Irishman said, "Is there much shooting up here? Grouse, I mean, and partridges, or whatever you have in this country?"

"I believe there are a few partridges," replied Templeton, "but I don't know. I'm not interested in shooting myself, and I don't believe I have handled a gun since I left the Army."

"Or a bomb?" said the Irishman swiftly, and Templeton started in spite of himself. The Irishman saw the start and instantly his alert manner subsided, and he lowered for the first time his sharp, bright little eyes. "I haven't seen a bomb myself," he went on easily, "since we signed the treaty and Ireland became a free country. Personally, I never want to see one again. Is there any fishing up here?"

Templeton was now watching the little man as closely as he had himself been watched. "I don't know," he answered slowly. "I am a stranger to these parts like yourself."

"Fishing is a mighty good sport," said the Irishman. "I've done a lot of fishing at one time or another. Did you ever see a big, black Irishman, with broad shoulders and black eyebrows, staying in this hotel?"

"Never," said Templeton, without the quiver of an eyelid. He was determined not to be drawn again.

"You know a lot more than you pretend," said the other quietly, and then he leant forward and tapped the young Englishman on the knee. "Take my advice and keep out of this," he said. "You are a nice boy and I wouldn't like to see you come to harm."

"I don't know what you mean," said Templeton stiffly.

"Well, don't say I didn't warn, you," said the Irishman, getting up. "It's a bad business, and you ought to keep out of it. Do you remember what happened after the Treaty was signed?"

"No," said Templeton.

"Well, it was Irishman against Irishman then and you English kept out of it. I advise you to do the same now," and with that he left the room.

Templeton's bewilderment had increased during this peculiar interview. After thinking hard for a few minutes he determined to stroll down towards the golf-course in order to meet Snell and tell him what had happened. On the doorstep he found both the Irishmen standing silently looking out at the sea. Neither of them paid the slightest attention to him and the one who had spoken to him in the smoking-room looked at him as if he had never seen him. Templeton determined not to be cut, and he paused and said, "It's a fine evening." They paid no attention to him and with a shrug of his shoulders he passed on.

As it chanced, Snell was holing out on the last green as he approached the links, and as soon as he and Armstrong had paid their caddies, the three of them wandered back to the hotel, while Templeton recounted the story of the interview. The side-road from the links met the main road a few hundred yards from the hotel. On reaching the junction of the two roads, Templeton suddenly halted and pointed to a tall figure which was striding in front of him towards the inn. "And there's the big black Irishman. I'll swear that's his back," he said. "I think we had better tell him that there are friends of his looking for him." They quickened their steps but were still a hundred yards behind him when he turned into the little enclosure which served as a front garden. The figures of the other two Irishmen were standing on the steps as Templeton had left them. As the tall man entered the garden the two men on the top of the steps simultaneously whipped out pistols and let loose a fusillade of shots. The tall man crumpled up and fell forward in a heap on the gravel.

Without an instant's delay, one of the attackers moved rapidly but without any sign of panic to their small motor-car which was standing in the road, while the other knelt over the body and deftly went through the pockets of the murdered man. Then in another second the two men were moving swiftly down the road in their car.

The whole drama had taken perhaps ten seconds. It was so sudden and unexpected that Templeton and his friends remained rooted to the spot for the brief interval that elapsed between the firing of the first shot and the sound of the small motor-car changing into second gear; then they sprang forward and ran to the assistance of the prostrate man. Pursuit of the car was out of the question. A single glance was sufficient for three ex-soldiers to realize that the man had been killed instantaneously. Windows were flung up in the hotel and anxious chambermaids peered out, while the landlord himself came, as rapidly as he could, round the outside of the hotel from the back entrance. In a few minutes the apparently deserted neighbourhood was peopled as if by magic with chauffeurs, golfers, caddies, hotel servants and casual passers-by.

Telephone messages were dispatched to the nearest police-station, and a doctor was found among the golfers. But the latter shook his head and said, after a quick examination: "It is not my business. It's a police affair."

The village constable arrived hot-foot on a bicycle and shook his head solemnly. He was not one of the traditional village policemen who are thirsting for glory and promotion, and who look upon a crime as a heaven-sent opportunity of proving their extraordinary abilities as a detective.

He was a quiet man, whose proudest boast was that in eighteen years' service in the force he had never arrested anyone, and only four times had he cautioned motorists for exceeding sixty miles an hour through the ten mile speed limit at the end of the village. His first action, therefore, was to telephone to the headquarters of the county constabulary, giving as full information as he could of the crime, and asking for assistance to be sent over as soon as possible.

It was past nine o'clock that evening when a fast motor arrived with the county officers. In the meantime, information about the small motor-car and a description of its occupants had been circulated to all police stations in the North-East of Scotland, and a keen and energetic watch was being kept.

There was no means of identifying the body of the dead man. The murderer had with amazing deftness made a clean sweep of any documents that he might have been carrying. His clothes were not marked.

Next morning the small motor-car in which the men had escaped was found abandoned in a field, and the farmer who lived in the neighbouring croft was able to tell the police that two days previously he had rented a large grass-field to a stranger, to be used as a landing-ground for an aeroplane. The aeroplane, said the farmer, had arrived the same afternoon, and he and his family had distinctly heard it leaving again late on the preceding night.

It subsequently turned out that people in Glasgow, Stranraer, and the northern parts of Ireland, had heard an aeroplane passing over during the night, and it was assumed that the two men had made good their escape into the fastnesses of Western Ireland. At any rate, nothing further was heard of them from that time on, and in spite of the most determined efforts by the police of the Irish Free State they vanished as completely as if they had never existed.

The murdered man was never identified. No one came forward to claim the considerable reward that was offered for his identification, and what was popularly called "The Irishmen's Battle" was ascribed to a personal vendetta such as used to flourish in Corsica, and such as English people assume still flourishes in Ireland.

CHAPTER IV

The Girl from the Factory on the Cliff

When the excitement of the chase, the police investigations, the inquiry by the ProcuratorFiscal, and the general buzz of gossip, theory and speculation had died down, Templeton found that his holiday was almost at an end. Another three days and he would be seated once more at his desk in the City corporation for which he worked. His thumb not yet allowing him to swing a golf-club, he determined to pay one last visit to the building on the top of the cliffs.

There was obviously some connection between it and the murdered man. He himself had seen and handled a bomb which Griffin was searching for; therefore there was a connection between the mysterious farmhouse and bombs. The murdered Irishman had visited the farmhouse. One of the murderers had spoken pointedly about bombs. Supposing that Griffin and his colleagues were manufacturing bombs to be used by anarchists; that would be a possible solution, but the difficulty was that nowadays anarchists hardly ever used bombs. "They are much more likely," reflected Templeton, "to use pamphlets. The bomb anarchist dates back to the days of the old Tsars in Russia."

Nor could the demand be sufficiently great to make such a place pay. On the other hand, it was out of the question that Griffin could he manufacturing bombs on a scale sufficiently large to equip even a small army. Templeton had been a divisional bombing officer at one time during the war, and he knew something of the number of bombs required by a modern army, even for one day's fighting. Griffin's establishment at the outside could hold enough bombs for the smallest of regiments engaged in the shortest of battles. And yet there was sufficient proof that the business, whatever it was, was of vital importance to somebody, if two men were prepared to commit murder in broad daylight over it. He determined, therefore, to make another visit, on the chance of finding some clue which might help him in connecting up the apparently inexplicable incidents of the last few weeks.

He set out, therefore, along the road where he had picked up the bomb, and proceeded as far as the cart-track. As soon as the cluster of buildings came into view he slipped behind the dyke and moved forward on hands and knees. When he came to the corner where the track turned and dipped, he halted and arranged a small loophole in the dyke, through which he could observe the buildings with his field-glasses.

For about twenty minutes he sat and watched, and then the door opened and the girl came out and began to walk with the same purposeful air towards him down the lane. Templeton felt extraordinarily embarrassed; he could not be certain whether she had seen him, and after a moment's hasty thought he came to the conclusion that her sallying from the house was a pure coincidence, and that his best plan would be to stay quiet and take the chance of being unobserved.

To his intense mortification, he heard the footsteps approach and then the girl's voice saying, "Don't you find it rather damp sitting in the field?" He rose to his feet, blushing, furiously angry with himself and with her.

"You seem determined to spy upon us," she went on.

"Are you afraid of being spied on?" he replied.

"Not in the least," she said with some asperity, "but it is an objectionable habit, and you certainly are the most incompetent spy I have ever seen."

Templeton felt himself blushing again, and he said, "How did you know I was here?"

"If you will turn your field-glasses so that the sun shines on them," she said, with a touch of scorn, "you can't expect us not to notice it. You were flashing away like a searchlight. For sheer incompetence you and your friends would be hard to beat."

There was a pause for a moment and then she said, "Don't you think your work in London is calling you?"

"Not for another forty-eight hours," said the young man, beginning to recover his composure. "Much may be done in forty-eight hours."

She looked up at him steadily and said, "What is it that you want here?"

"I am interested," he said, "in bombs and Irishmen and the migration of fishes."

"I cannot make out," said the girl, "whether you are the biggest fool in Scotland or not. I suppose it would be no use asking you to come and have tea with me?"

32

"Is that your parlour," said Templeton, "because if so I should prefer not to play the part of the fly."

A faint tinge of colour appeared in the dead white of her cheeks. "What do you think I would do to you?" she asked.

"I don't know," said Templeton with a laugh, "but it seems a very unhealthy neighbourhood."

"Unhealthy," she said slowly. "That is about the best description that could possibly be given to it. Don't say I didn't warn you," and she turned to go.

"In story-books," he said, "the beautiful heroine always warns the hero to fly and save his life."

She smiled a slightly mischievous smile. "Casting yourself for the part of hero?"

"Every inch a hero," responded Templeton, puffing out his chest and pulling down his coat. "And you are the heroine," he added gallantly.

"Well, I fear that you've already gone too far. I doubt if you could save your life even by flying."

"Naughty, naughty," said the young man, shaking his forefinger at her. "Making threats like that. Really, I'm surprised."

She gave an almost imperceptible shrug of her neat shoulders. Then she held out a small hand and said: "Good-bye and good luck. You'll need all you can get."

"Tut, tut!" said Templeton with a laugh. The girl frowned, turned sharply on her heel, and marched, head in air, back to the farm.

He found Snell in the smoking-room and recounted the conversation. "There's nothing for it," he concluded, "but to visit the place by night and go up that path to the house. Do you want to come?"

"You bet I do," was the instant reply, "and Armstrong will have to come too to row. Count us both in."

The evening found the three friends at work oiling the oars of the rowing boat which they had again hired, and filling their flasks with the landlord's excellent whisky.

Towards midnight they slipped quietly out of the hotel and proceeded, by three different routes, to the harbour, taking the utmost precautions to see that they were not followed. It was one of those long summer nights in the North of Scotland when the sun hardly seems to sink at all, and even at half-past twelve there was a distinct light in the western sky, either of the setting or of the rising sun, but by keeping close inshore, the three adventurers succeeded in hiding themselves and their boat in the complete darkness thrown by the shadow of the cliffs. They pulled silently up the coast, Templeton again steering, until they rounded the first of the promontories that guarded the narrow cove. They halted the boat at the end of the promontory and waited for a long five minutes to see whether there was a watchman who had observed their approach. Everything, however, was quiet by the sandy beach, but a light in a window of the farmhouse showed that the little community had not yet retired to bed.

At last Templeton gave the word and they pulled silently in to the shore, moored the boat to the little rowing boat which lay high and dry on the sand, and crept towards the path which led up the cliffs. In single file they moved slowly up, Templeton leading, Snell behind him, and Armstrong bringing up the rear.

There was no sign of a sentry or watcher of any sort, and the three men reached the top of the path unhindered. There they found a short patch of grass, no more than fifteen feet in length, between themselves and the lighted window of the farmhouse. They had not realized how close the building was to the edge of the cliff.

Templeton crept forward to listen at the window, the other two remaining at the head of the path. The window was open and it was perfectly easy to hear every syllable that was uttered in the room. Templeton listened, and could hardly believe his ears. He had expected to overhear some dark conspiracy, or at least some information which would help him to clear up the tangle. Instead of that, he found himself eavesdropping at a harmless and quiet game of family bridge. There was not a sound in the room except the shuffle of the cards and the quiet voices of the players.

For about ten minutes he waited, and was then on the point of creeping back and heading the retreat to the boat when it occurred to him that it was unusual for people to play bridge in a country farmhouse after one o'clock in the morning. It was possible, he thought, that they were whiling away the time and waiting for something which they expected to happen. Just as this thought crossed his mind, he heard an electric bell ring and then a voice obviously answering the telephone. He heard someone say, "Wait a minute while I write it down." Then came a long silence, during which the speaker at the other end of the telephone was doing all the talking while the person at the farmhouse end was writing it down.

Then a voice said, "Is that all? Very well, good night"; and there was the click of the telephone receiver being put back in its place. "This is what Morton says," went on the voice.

"George Templeton is in business in London, in the 'Anglo-Siamese Trading Corporation.' About twenty-eight, unmarried, not much sense.

Henry Snell is twenty-nine and in the Home Office; looked upon as very promising.

Armstrong is a stockbroker, and Morton can't find out much about him except that he is unintelligent and is a champion thrower of the hammer and an international Rugby football player.

He could not find any apparent connection between them and Scotland Yard, but he is going to telephone again tomorrow."

A much deeper voice spoke for the first time and said, "I don't much care about Mr Henry Snell's profession. A man from the Home Office is just the sort of person that might be sent up here. We had better take steps about it. Switch those lights out, will you?"

Templeton realized that he would not likely hear more, and began to back towards the path, when he heard a slight exclamation behind him, and then the sound of a stone leaping and bounding from rock to rock down the cliff to the beach. He held his breath for a moment, hoping that it had not been heard, but there was a sudden silence inside the farmhouse and then a voice said, "What the devil was that?" and an inside door was flung open and footsteps ran towards the outer door.

Templeton, sprang up and ran for the path, and the three friends fled as fast as they could towards their boat. Their breakneck descent of the steep, narrow path in the darkness was achieved at the risk of their lives. The pursuers, who knew more of the risks, followed more slowly, and the big boat had almost rounded the promontory before the pursuers reached the foot, but if the inhabitants of the farmhouse had been unwilling to risk their necks in racing down the path, they made up for lost time by the energy and speed of their actions when once they had got down. The cove was lit up with a blaze of revolver flashes. Chips of wood were flicked off the rowing boat, and the rowers were splashed by spurts of water thrown up by the bullets. But it was too dark for accurate shooting and the next moment a friendly rock was between the boat and the battery of pistols. As soon as they were round the headland, Templeton steered for the land. "We can't do much when that motor-boat gets started," he muttered. "What a devilish business."

They pulled for the shore and by great good fortune chanced on a narrow section where a long grass field stretched down to the edge of the sea, instead of the almost perpendicular cliffs on each side.

As soon as the keel touched the sand, the three men tumbled out and began hurrying up the steep grass slope. As they did so, the motorboat came round the headland and began to sweep the sea and the coast with a small searchlight. The beam swung round and quickly picked up the rowing-boat; another moment and it was concentrated on the dark figures struggling up the hill. "That's done us," muttered Armstrong, but there was no more firing.

The motor-boat gradually crept towards the shore while the searchlight followed the fugitives up the hill. When they reached the top, they simultaneously sank down to recover their breath and take stock of the situation. Suddenly Snell pointed towards the road. He was too much out of breath to speak. A motor-car was cruising slowly towards the main road with headlights fully switched on. In the back seat a man was standing holding a powerful electric torch. When the car reached the main road, it turned to the left and went slowly in the direction of the village and the hotel.

From the direction of the farmhouse came another ray of light which soon resolved itself into an electric torch in the hands of a pedestrian.

Looking back, they could see figures landing from the motor-boat. "We can't stay here," said Templeton. "And we can't go back or forwards," said Armstrong grimly. "Then let's go sideways," said Snell in a cheerful whisper, and he led the way on hands and knees, just below the level of the skyline, towards the rocky cliffs which terminated the grassy slope a few yards away. He chose a path at random, and led the way gingerly from rock to rock, feeling his way in the darkness. A few yards took them to a sort of rocky nest, screened from view from above and from the sea and providing just enough room for them to sit down.

They settled themselves down as comfortably as they could to wait for developments. It was not long before the landing party from the motorboat made the laborious ascent to the skyline, where they halted. There were three of them, and a minute later a hoarse whisper from the landward side showed that they had established contact with their friends, either from the motor-car or from the search party on foot.

There was a whispered consultation and then a fifth man joined them. He talked a little louder than the others, and the three friends distinctly overheard the words, "Wait till dawn. Tom has gone to cut them off from the hotel"; and another voice said, "Not going to risk my neck on the rocks." After a little more whispering the group split up, the landing party returning to the motor-boat. Then came the sound of the engines starting, and Snell, peering through a chink in the rocks, could see below him the outline of the motor-boat slowly returning to the cove. Behind it was the dark shape of another boat. "By Jove," he said, "they've pinched our boat.

The dirty dogs! We're like Napoleon in Egypt — retreat by sea cut off. What's the next move?"

"It seems to me," said Templeton after a moment, "that we have three possible courses: either to wait for the dawn, in which case they will find us at once, or else to make a dash for the hotel, and that's rather a hopeless business if the car has gone down the road to wait for us. The other thing would be for one of us to try to get out and go to the nearest farmhouse for help. All we have to do is to bring a couple of farm hands over here; there won't be any violence if there are independent witnesses standing about."

"That's the best plan — the last one," whispered Snell. "We'll toss for it. The odd man out goes for help."

Armstrong and Templeton tossed heads and Snell tails. "Cheerio," he said. "I'll be back in half an hour." He pulled up his coat-collar and slipped quietly round the rock along the path by which they had come.

"Take care of yourself, Harry," muttered Armstrong.

The other two waited; there was dead silence except for the murmur of the waves below. The light was already beginning to come, and they realized that the search would start again at any moment. Suddenly there was a loud shout, followed by a wild scream which echoed from rock to rock and set the gulls wheeling and crying.

"What in the name of the fiend was that?" whispered Templeton.

"The first was Henry," said Armstrong, who had started up, "but not the second, I'll swear to that. They were different voices."

"I wish to heaven we were armed," said Templeton. "I don't like this at all. Anyway, there's no good sitting here. I'm afraid Snell has been caught."

"You lead on," said Armstrong.

"Our only chance," said Templeton, "and it's a damned poor one at that, is to go straight back to the cove by the rocks, work our way round the other headland and try to get up the cliffs on the north side of the cove. They will expect us to make a dash for the hotel and they won't be looking for us in that direction."

Crouching low, they slipped down as rapidly as they could to the edge of the sea and began to climb from rock to rock out to the point of the headland from which they had originally surveyed the mysterious farmhouse. The tide was out and they made rapid progress. On reaching the place where Armstrong's unfortunate fall had first roused the attention of the watchers in the farm, they made a cautious examination of the sandy beach, the path above it and the buildings at the top. There appeared to be no movement and there were no signs of a sentry anywhere.

"Come on," said Templeton. "We must risk it," and they made for the shore, again from rock to rock, on the inside of the headland. About half-way Templeton stopped, with a half-stifled exclamation. "Is that Snell?" he said hoarsely.

Armstrong, who had been a little behind, came up beside him and looked for a moment at a twisted and shattered body that lay face downward like a huge grotesque starfish in front of them. He shuddered for a moment and then said decisively: "No, that's not Henry. It must be the man who screamed." He pulled out his handkerchief and wiped his brow.

Templeton could see that the big, stolid footballer was profoundly anxious for his friend. He turned the body over. "It's the lorry driver," he said, "that I saw on the first day. Snell must have run into him and he got tumbled over. Let's get on quickly."

It was full daylight by the time they had rounded the second headland and had once more completed a painful and laborious ascent of the cliffs. At the top they found a long, low stone dyke running at right angles to the sea-coast, marking the boundary between one farm and another. It afforded excellent cover from any possible watchers in the upper storey of the buildings at Gulls' Cove. Half a mile away, across open country, was the nearest croft, and it was towards this objective that Templeton and Armstrong turned.

They had hardly gone a hundred yards along the wall when the sound of a powerful motorengine brought them to a halt. An aeroplane came slowly from the south and began to make wide sweeps at a height of only three or four hundred feet, in a circle of which the cove was approximately the centre.

Both Templeton and Armstrong had learned the art of taking cover in the war, and especially the art of hiding from aeroplanes, the essence of which is never to show one's face. An upturned face is the one thing that the aviator looks for and recognizes. The two men, therefore, lay at full length beside the dyke, until the aeroplane was making one of its wider sweeps, and they could advance a few yards before it returned. In this way they made a certain amount of progress without being detected until they suddenly came to the end of the dyke and found that there was at least a quarter of a mile of open field between themselves and the farm.

As a dash across the open space was out of the question they decided to follow another dyke which led in a northerly direction towards the stretch of moor. The drawback was that it took them away from the haven of refuge in the croft, but it seemed better to take the risk of finding another farm rather than try the suicidal rush across the bare ground. They continued their spasmodic advance until they came to the end of the second dyke and the edge of the moor. There was nothing but open country on all sides, and the only available cover was the whin and broom bushes on the moor and the occasional clumps of long grass and reeds which marked the winter bogs.

They looked back. On the only two roads that were visible, motor-cars were slowly patrolling, while men were silhouetted against the skyline on the top of the cliffs. There was nothing for it but to continue the flight across the moor. Taking advantage of every ditch and whin bush, the two men continued to put as great a distance as possible between themselves and their pursuers.

Once the aeroplane circled the moor while the fugitives lay partially concealed among a clump of reeds, then it wheeled and made off towards the south, wheeled again and returned to the moor, flying not more than twenty feet above the ground. It passed directly above the clump of reeds and the next moment it turned abruptly and began a long spiral climb and then, at the height of about fifteen hundred feet, patrolled the moor backwards and forwards.

"I don't like this," said Templeton. "They must have spotted us. If he has got wireless on board he'll send a message to the farmhouse. Can you see the farm from here? Don't show your face."

Armstrong turned round in the reeds and looked back.

"Yes, I can," he said; "and I can see several people running. They have got another car there."

"That will be it," said Templeton. "The aeroplane has wirelessed to them. Well, there's no need for concealment now. Come on." Rising to their feet they threw off all attempt at taking cover, and set off at a brisk trot across the moor. The aeroplane descended a few hundred feet and cruised above them. Looking over their shoulders they could see a motor-car moving along the road on the side of the moor furthest from the sea, on a course parallel to their own.

"I'm getting a bit fed up with this," said Armstrong. "Running and climbing and being shot at. I wonder what has happened to Snell?"

"Save your breath," said Templeton, "you'll need it all before we've finished," and they went on running in silence.

The drone of the aeroplane overhead was the only indication on the lovely summer's morning that there was anything amiss.

Then they had their first piece of good luck. They had been pounding up a long, gradual slope, and when they reached the top they ran full tilt into a small party of men with guns in their hands.

"What the devil is all this!" exclaimed one of them, and the party came to a standstill and stared at the two runners, who certainly presented a peculiar spectacle. A night spent in climbing rocks, in furious rowing, in running, and creeping on all fours across fields and moors, does not improve the appearance of the clothes.

"It's not so bad as it looks," said Templeton, gasping for breath; "or rather it's a great deal worse."

"That explains everything," said the other dryly.

"It's a long story," said Templeton, "but I would very much like to tell it to you."

"Well, you have the whole day before you," said the other. "Take your time. You seem a little out of breath."

"The main thing," said Templeton, "is that we are going to stick to you like limpets."

"That's very flattering," put in another member of the shooting-party. "I don't know what we have done to deserve the honour. It's time we were moving on, Alastair, if we are to do any shooting before breakfast."

The man addressed as Alastair was the one who had spoken first, and he looked curiously at the two runners. "There's more in this than meets the eye," he said. "You look like escaped convicts, if I may say so, and you talk like Oxford men."

"Cambridge," said Armstrong, who had been standing stolidly beside Templeton.

"I say," said one of the strangers, turning to Armstrong curiously, "why aren't you out of breath too?"

"Training for Rugger," was the laconic answer.

"The fact is," said Templeton rather more cheerfully, "we don't like the people in that aeroplane, and they don't like us. That's partly our trouble."

Everyone instinctively looked up. The aeroplane had again descended and was now about five hundred feet above them.

"My name is Chisholm — Alastair Chisholm," said the first man suddenly. "I think we won't do any shooting this morning. There is my house over there. Let's go back and have a bath and something to eat."

He was a young man, not more than thirty-five, with a cheerful red face, and his companions consisted of two other men of about the same age and three gamekeepers.

40

In half an hour Templeton was recounting the whole affair from the beginning to an enthralled audience at the breakfast-table of Sir Alastair Chisholm. The aeroplane had vanished, but a powerful motor-car had taken up its position on the top of the hill a short distance away, whence it commanded an excellent view of the house.

CHAPTER V

Sir Alastair Chisholm

At the end of the story Sir Alastair lit a cigarette and turned to his guests. "The perfect host, you see," he said. "I not only provide shooting and fishing, but a complete melodrama as well. All this is carefully organized and naturally I have spared no expense. The first thing is to get in touch with the police. In a real melodrama we would, of course, keep the police out of it, solve the mystery ourselves, bring to book a gang of desperate criminals and all marry the most incredibly beautiful crookesses, but somehow it seems difficult in real life. There's something, for instance, very unpleasant about that car standing up there," and he pointed out of the window.

"And there's only one crookess, apparently," put in one of the other men gloomily.

"I quite agree with you," said Templeton to Chisholm. "I have had quite enough of this amateur sleuthing, especially as most of the sleuthing seems to be done by the other side. I always thought that in things like this the amateurs did all the pursuing."

"There's just one thing," interposed one of the shooting party. "What are you going to tell the police, and what crime are you going to charge these people with?"

"Oh, I say!" protested Chisholm. "Just because you have been called to the Bar, Charlie, you needn't pretend to be so superior. There are enough crimes here to fill the Newgate calendar. By the way, have I introduced you? The gent who has just spoken is Mr Pollock — Mr Charles Pollock, a man with a most offensively legal mind. The youth opposite who spends three-quarters of the day asleep is Mr Gardiner, usually called the Oyster."

"My name is Templeton, and this is Mr Armstrong."

"That's where I've seen you," said the barrister. "At Twickenham, surely?" Armstrong nodded.

"Weren't you playing in the English scrum against Scotland in the Calcutta Cup?"

"Yes."

"I am honoured, sir," said Chisholm solemnly. Armstrong said nothing, but continued to attack a vast plate of bacon and eggs.

"To revert to the Newgate calendar," said the barrister. He was a tall, thin young man, dark, with a fine, intelligent face and a ready smile. Templeton put him down as a highbrow with a sense of humour. Chisholm appeared to be a hearty creature of unlimited kindness and good-fellowship. The third member of the party was small and slightly built, with small hands and feet, fair hair, a face like a cherub, and the roundest of round blue eyes when they were open; as a rule they were half-closed.

"You say there are enough crimes to fill it," went on Pollock. "Well, what are they? Look at it from the point of view of the other chaps. Suppose they really are scientists working on some immensely important and valuable investigation; these three lads butt in after dark; they are mistaken for burglars and the scientists fire at them. That might possibly form a police-court case, but I think there is no doubt they would be acquitted. If not, it would be a very small matter — protecting one's property after dark."

"But what about the disappearance of our friend Snell?" said Templeton.

"Yes," echoed Armstrong, "what about that?"

"Well, has he disappeared?" said the barrister. "For all you know he may be sitting in the smoking-room of the hotel with his feet on the mantelpiece, drinking whisky and soda."

"Not at this hour of the morning," growled Armstrong.

"Well, then, a cup of tea. And there's another point. Suppose they are harmless scientists, and suppose your Mr Snell has pushed one of them over the cliffs on their own premises at night. That would look uncommonly like murder."

Armstrong sat up abruptly and scowled, and Templeton said, "By Jove! I never thought of that. But then — the bomb?"

The barrister shrugged his shoulders. "You can't produce it in court, I fancy, and you are not quite certain yourself that it was a bomb. You said it was much too light."

"It certainly was light," said Templeton. "Too light for an ordinary bomb, but it might be something special."

"Well," said the barrister. "It's not my business, but it doesn't look to me as if you had much to go on. Apparently the three of you have forcibly entered other people's premises at night, and at least one of you may have possibly committed a murder."

Chisholm broke in excitedly. "That's all bunkum, Charlie, and you know it. It's only your infernal legal mind that likes to make difficulties. What about the pursuit in the aeroplane, and what about that car out there now? What about the murder of the Irishman?"

"Oh, I agree it looks fishy," said the barrister.

"Fishy!" Chisholm almost exploded. "I should jolly well think it does look fishy."

The third member of the shooting party at this point murmured something inaudible. Chisholm turned on him with a shout of delight. "The Oyster has woken up at last," he cried. "Come on, Oyster, what's the trouble now? Bring out today's great pearl."

The young man raised his voice a little and murmured, "It seems to me to depend on whether Mr Henry Snell has returned to his hotel or not."

"What a brain!" exclaimed Chisholm admiringly, and he seized the telephone. In a few minutes he was speaking to a hotel boots who assured him that Mr Snell had not returned, neither had the other two gentlemen who had gone out late on the previous evening in a boat. The boots assured him that nothing out of the common had occurred throughout the night at the hotel; he himself had been on duty all the time. A motor-car had broken down just outside, shortly after one o'clock, and the chauffeur had spent several hours trying to repair it; but apart from that nothing had happened.

The young man called the Oyster, who had been gazing out of the window with a rapt and absent expression, spoke again. "There's a sportsman climbing one of your telegraph poles," he observed mildly. The next moment the baronet broke into a torrent of abuse against the telephone system for having cut him off in the middle of a conversation, but his shouts and bangs on the instrument produced not the slightest result.

"I think," said the Oyster again, "that the sportsman has cut your wire."

Chisholm's indignation instantly vanished and he became thoroughly alert. "Come on. To business," he said. "We must get in touch with the Inverness police at once."

"We'd better not put all our eggs in one basket," said Templeton. "I suggest that Armstrong and I make a dash for it while you get your wire mended. If you don't hear from us in, say, six hours, you can then have a shot at it. If you want to be mixed up in it," he added.

"I should say so," said the baronet fervently. It was arranged that Chisholm's car should leave the house, driven by his chauffeur and containing two of the gamekeepers, carefully muffled and wrapped up, in the back seat. It was to go as fast as possible to Tomnarroch, the nearest station on the Inverness line. As soon as the pursuers had been drawn off to follow this car, the old Ford which carried the luggage was to go with Templeton and Armstrong to the station of Auchterless, beyond Tomnarroch and nearer Inverness.

The strategy was successful. The car which had been stationary at the top of the hill followed at a discreet interval to Tomnarroch, while the Ford clattered off unperceived in the other direction in time to catch a slow train to Inverness.

Installed in a first-class carriage, the only one in the little train, Templeton, for the first time in a good many hours, was able to relax his attention and drop off into a doze. Armstrong remained doggedly awake. The train jogged slowly from Station to station, stopping at each for what seemed hours, but was actually several minutes. Templeton was aroused from his doze by Armstrong's hand on his knee. "There's something funny going on here," he said. "We've been in this station nearly ten minutes." Templeton looked out. It was a tiny wayside station. Two or three houses were within sight, but there was no village. The stationmaster, who acted as ticket collector, booking-clerk, porter and signalman, was standing talking to the engine-driver.

"He has walked the whole length of the train," said Armstrong, "looking into each carriage." At that moment the engine whistled and the train started off again with a jerk. The stationmaster hurried back into his office.

"I don't like the look of it," said Templeton. "I think there will be trouble at the next station." The train went even slower than usual, and Templeton seriously considered the possibility of dropping off and risking a sprained ankle. But just as he was weighing up the situation, the brakes went on again and the train clanked into another station. His worst fears were realized, for on the platform was the station-master and an individual who was obviously the local policeman, and two men dressed as farm labourers. As the train pulled up, the party made a dash for the first-class carriage. The station-master and the policeman began speaking excitedly and simultaneously, the latter waving a telegram. Templeton at first pretended not to understand what they wanted, but the meaning was made clear as soon as the policeman gave the station-master a free hand.

The telegram had come, he explained, from the station of Tomnarroch, containing an accurate description of the two men and instructions to detain them until the arrival of detectives, who were following in a motor.

They descended on the platform; Templeton was thinking furiously. There were two possibilities: either information had been lodged against Snell and themselves for the murder of the lorry-driver who had fallen over the cliff, in which case it really was the police who were after them. If that was so, the best policy was to wait. On the other hand, it was far more likely to be the occupants of the Gulls' Cove Farm, in which case the best policy was to get away. Once in the hands of that gentry, the outlook would not be very bright.

Armstrong was clearly not thinking at all. He was scowling fearfully and his fists were clenched. At any moment, Templeton thought, he might break out into physical violence. He turned to the policeman and said, "May I telephone?"

"You may not," said the policeman. "Will you telephone for me?"

"I will not."

"Will you send a message for me to Sir Alastair Chisholm?"

"You can do that from Inverness gaol."

"But it is vitally important that I should do it now."

"Umph!" was the only answer.

"Look here," said Templeton, "I have every reason to suppose that that telegram is a bogus message."

"Shut your head," roared the policeman, "or you'll get a ding on the side of it that'll shut it for ye. Ye're arrested. Dinna forget that. We'll lock the blackguards in the waiting-room," he said to the station-master, and with the assistance of their plain-clothes allies, he began to shepherd his prisoners to the waiting-room. The station-master turned round to signal to the engine-driver that all was clear, and the engine gave a whistle and started. The whistle was apparently the signal that Armstrong had been waiting for. With a perfect right-handed swing he knocked the farm labourer nearest him spinning across the platform, and with a shout of "Go for the train," he dashed into the station telegraph room, picked up a chair, and began to wreck the instruments. With a howl of rage, the policeman spun round and dashed in pursuit, and the other labourer and the station-master ran in after him. Templeton, left alone on the platform, started to go to the rescue of his friend, and then realized that it would be far wiser to take his advice; he made a sprint for the moving train, opened the door of a carriage and tumbled in. The last thing he saw of the station, as the train puffed round the bend, was a heap of human beings on the platform, and a number of legs and arms kicking in all directions.

Luckily he had tumbled into an empty carriage and he had time in the interval before the next station to consider rapidly a plan of campaign. For the time being, at any rate, he was free from pursuit, assuming that Armstrong had succeeded in smashing the station telephone and telegraph instruments. "From what little I have seen of Armstrong," Templeton murmured to himself with satisfaction, "I should think he has smashed the place to splinters. One of the bulldog breed is Armstrong. I might get out and telephone for help to Chisholm. No, that's no good; his telephone wire is cut. The best thing I can do is to sit here and go to Inverness."

The slow train at last puffed its way into Inverness station and Templeton drove in a cab to the office of the County Constabulary. He was received by the Chief Constable himself, a man who resembled rather a country gentleman or a retired military officer than a policeman. He listened politely to Templeton's story and at the end he said, "I can confirm a part of your story at any rate. I had a mysterious telephone message from a local constable, saying that one of the wanted men had escaped but that the other one had been taken into custody by the detectives. As I knew nothing of the matter and had sent out no detectives, I was naturally somewhat puzzled, but your story explains it.

"It appears that after your friend was finally captured by the local warriors, and apparently it wasn't an easy matter, he was kept in the waiting-room until a motor-car came to fetch him. He went quite quietly and there was no further violence. I must find out whether the people in the car presented any credentials to show that they were policemen. But I should think it unlikely, if your story is correct. And now, sir," he went on, "what do you want me to do?"

"To do!" echoed Templeton in surprise. "I want my friends back."

"Quite so," murmured the Chief Constable. "Perhaps they will come back when they want to."

"But they have been kidnapped, abducted, or whatever you call it!"

"The report," answered the imperturbable official, "says that your friend went quietly into the motor-car without any fuss or violence."

Templeton stared at him. "Do you mean that it wasn't a case of kidnapping?"

The official laughed. "If I had to pursue everyone who got quietly into motor-cars, I should have a fairly busy time."

"But what about Snell?"

"Is there any evidence that he has been kidnapped?" asked the Chief Constable.

"Suppose he knocked that man down the cliffs, and then got frightened and lost his head. He might be hiding for fear of being arrested."

"But all the other things," cried Templeton. "The bomb and the shooting and the aeroplane!" The other man got up and patted Templeton in a kindly way on the shoulder. "My dear young friend," he said, "you are letting your imagination run away with you. If you will take my advice, you will go back to London to your work. If neither of your friends turn up in the course of the next day or two, you should then go to Scotland Yard and lodge an official report that they are missing. I don't mind betting you a small sum that you will find them in London before you, and that the whole thing can be explained."

He held out his hand, and Templeton had no alternative but to accept the hint that the interview was over. The Chief Constable took him as far as the door of the building, talking courteously about the weather, the prospects of the harvest, the shooting, and a golf tournament that was shortly to be held in the neighbourhood.

Templeton stood on the steps of the police station in a bewildered and indignant frame of mind. He was thoroughly angry at the stupid and unintelligent attitude of the Chief Constable, and he was completely puzzled as to what he ought to do next. For one thing he was quite uncertain whether he had shaken off the attention of his pursuers, but he had already had ample evidence that they were energetic and rapid in their movements and were well equipped with mechanical transport.

Three possible courses seemed to be open: to return to London as the Chief Constable had advised; to go back to the hotel and begin the search for his two friends in that neighbourhood; or to double back to Sir Alastair Chisholm and make use of his newly-found and enthusiastic allies. Whichever he did, it was imperative that he should make a move at once before the pursuers picked up the trail that they had lost. He looked round, therefore, for a cab in which to return to the station when suddenly he heard a soft voice behind him murmur, "Dear me, if it isn't Mr Templeton." He wheeled round to find himself face to face with the girl from the Farm at the Gulls' Cove.

CHAPTER VI

The Inquisitive
Mr Templeton

"Still inquisitive, Mr Templeton?" asked the girl in a soft voice, looking up at him from under the brim of her hat. She might have been an old friend whom he had not seen for years. There was not a trace of embarrassment or shyness. "What are you looking for this time?"

"I am looking for my friends," he answered. Although he instinctively disliked the girl he could not help admitting to himself that she was a very lovely person and, in addition, the possessor of an apparently cast-iron nerve. She looked so feminine, so small, so appealing for protection; and yet Templeton had only to glance at her clear and resolute eyes and her complete self-confidence to realize that if either of them needed protection it was himself.

"Looking for your friends," she echoed, "and so of course you come straight to the police. Very natural indeed and very wise. Have they caught him yet?"

"Caught who?"

"Caught whom is better grammar. I mean your friend Mr Snell."

"And why should they want my friend Mr Snell?"

Her blue eyes opened wide and she gazed at him with an air of innocent amazement and alarm. "Really, Mr Templeton, what a hideous desperado you must be. I am positively frightened to be in your company even in a public street."

Templeton thought he had never seen anyone who looked less frightened.

"Your friend goes and throws a man over a cliff so that he breaks his neck and then you're surprised at the idea that the police might have something to say about it. Where have you lived all your life? In Arizona? Mr Templeton, I'm ashamed of you."

He grinned broadly.

"It's easy for you to smile," she went on. "It'll be different for Mr Snell. He won't find it a laughing matter. There are plenty of witnesses. We all saw it happen. A dastardly and unprovoked attack."

"There may be plenty of witnesses, but I doubt if they're the sort who will cut much ice in the witness-box. I shouldn't think they'd care to go into a police-court at all."

"Well, well, we shall see," said the girl. "He laughs last, and so on. In the meantime what about the police? Are they going to help you?"

"What is your name?" asked Templeton suddenly, ignoring her question. For the first time the girl gave the faintest start, a mere flicker of the eyelids, but enough to show that she had been taken unawares.

"Don't be so direct," she said; "you nearly startled me into . . ."

"Telling the truth," he prompted, and she smiled sweetly.

"My name is Blake, Susan Blake."

"Susan is good," replied Templeton with a grin. "You look like a Susan. Nice domestic sort of girl, sewing shirts for soldiers and all that sort of thing. Look here, Susan, what's all this about? I'm completely at sea."

She hesitated for a moment and then said: "It's a long story. I can't tell you while we are standing in the street. Come and have lunch with me in one of these hotels and I'll tell you as much as I can."

Templeton pointed down the road. "That looks quite a good hotel. Let's try it," and they turned down the street.

"Why did they kill the Irishman?" said Templeton; and again the girl started a little.

"Because they didn't like him, I suppose," she said lightly. "What makes you think that I would know?" She looked up at him with an air of innocent inquiry.

"He visited your house."

"A business acquaintance of my father's," she said. "We were all sorry that he was killed." She broke off and pointed to a coat-of-arms above a doorway. "That's picturesque, don't you think?" she said.

Templeton turned to look at it. It so chanced that the shop below the coat-of-arms had a long mirror beside its window, and the young man saw, at the same moment, the reflection of the girl making a movement of her hand that looked suspiciously like a signal. He turned back to her and said, "A beautiful coat-of-arms. Can you make out the crest?"

"It's rather worn," she murmured. "Here's the hotel."

"It looked to me," said Templeton, "like a spider rampant and a fly. I'm afraid lunch is off, Susan." He took off his hat and bowed.

The girl laughed cheerfully. "How clever of you to notice. I was over-confident. I lose a free lunch; life is very hard, Mr Templeton. Won't you even stand me a cocktail?" But Templeton was already striding rapidly in the direction of the station.

As he reached the corner of the street, he glanced over his shoulder and saw the girl still standing in the entrance of the hotel. A shabbily dressed man shuffled up to her, paused for a brief instant, and then came sidling down towards him. A second man was converging on him from the other side of the road. Templeton turned and took to his heels. At the next corner he took another glance and saw that the pursuers on foot were not in sight, but a taxi had turned the corner from the hotel and in front of it a small man with a red moustache and a face like a rat was bicycling along furiously.

Templeton was still some distance ahead when he ran into the station. He dashed round the booking-office on to the platform. There was no sign of any activity, either of trains arriving or departing. He seized a porter and breathlessly demanded, "When's the next train?"

"Where to?" said the porter. "Anywhere," he replied.

The porter looked surprised but answered politely that there was not a train to anywhere for the next twenty minutes.

Templeton sprinted to a door marked "Luggage only," sprang nimbly over the trunks and handbags that were strewn on the floor, and out into the street again. His one object now was to find a garage where he could hire a car. Looking over his shoulder again, he could see that his departure from the station had been observed and the pursuit was in full cry.

The chances of a man on foot are poor against a motor or a bicycle and it was as a last resort that he rushed into the Post Office and dived to a telephone box.

"This will give me a breathing space," he said to himself. "They surely won't try to dig me out of this in full view of all those good citizens buying stamps."

Two of the pursuers lounged into the Post Office, the shabbily-dressed man and another whom he had not seen before. One pretended to write a telegram, while the other walked to the counter. Then the little, rat-faced man slipped in and took up a strategic position at the door. Somehow he looked much more dangerous and intelligent than the other two. He took off his hat and scratched his head thoughtfully, and Templeton could see that he had flaming red hair and very bright eyes and a quick, unobtrusive manner. He felt that he was the opponent to reckon with.

He lifted the receiver, and after a moment's hesitation decided to try to get through to Sir Alastair Chisholm, on the chance that the wire had been mended. But there was no answer from Chisholm's number. Templeton then tried the Chief Constable's office, but that worthy had gone out to lunch, and his story that he was penned up in a public telephone box by three desperadoes who were at that moment buying stamps in the Post Office, was received by a subordinate with a certain amount of amused scepticism.

He hung up the receiver and thought for a moment. "I wonder if I really have lost my head," he thought. "After all, what can they do in broad daylight in the Post Office?"

He threw open the door of the box and stepped boldly out. Immediately the man who had been writing a telegram stepped straight up to the box as though to telephone. He stopped beside Templeton. "Come along with me," he murmured. At the same time he poked the muzzle of a pistol into the young man's waistcoat. It was a shadowy corner of the Post Office and the movement passed unobserved. The man from the counter sidled up towards them and began to talk in a hoarse, confidential whisper about race-horses. They looked like a group of acquaintances.

"Don't make a sound," said the man with the pistol menacingly.

Templeton looked wildly round, but could see no help. The little red-haired man had vanished. The taller of his two assailants took him by the arm in a friendly way, holding the pistol in his coat-pocket with the other hand, and edged him towards the door. The other man followed behind. A taxi was waiting, and in another second Templeton would have shared the fate of Armstrong and been kidnapped in broad daylight, apparently of his own free will. But at the door of the Post Office a diversion occurred. A huge Highland policeman in uniform dropped a heavy hand on the shoulder of the first of the two men. "I'll trouble you to take a little walk with me," he said, in a musical Highland accent.

"What the devil do you mean?" said the other, going pale and cringing.

"Unlawful possession of fire-arms," said the policeman. "Come quietly or there will be trouble."

The man looked round for a second and then tried to make a bolt for it. But the policeman's enormous hand closed on the scruff of his neck, and he picked him up and shook him like a rat. At the same moment, two other policemen hove into sight and the capture was complete. "How did you know I had a pistol?" said the prisoner in a very aggrieved tone.

"You mind your own business," said the policeman. "Come along this way." Templeton looked round. The second man had bolted and the rat-faced man was nowhere to be seen. He fell into step behind the three policemen, determined to remain within a yard of such strong and purposeful keepers of the King's peace until he could find a garage. Within ten minutes he was sitting back in a powerful Fiat motor-car, and was being driven rapidly in the direction of Sir Alastair Chisholm's house. At intervals he murmured to himself, "That was a narrow squeak."

Templeton got a great welcome from the three young men on his return, and his story aroused even the Oyster to a faint show of enthusiasm.

When he had finished, Pollock the barrister turned to his friends and said, "There's one very curious point about all this. I have no doubt it has escaped your attention, and I need hardly say that it has not escaped mine."

"Oh, come off it, Charlie," said Chisholm; "Tell us today's great thought."

"The point is this," proceeded Pollock unmoved. "These three young men are being pursued because they have acquired some information which apparently some other people want suppressed. They come to this house and presumably tell us all about it. Therefore it would be reasonable to suppose that we now have the information that they have, and yet the pursuit goes on after the original three and no attention is paid to us. Therefore, I ask you what sort of information is it that is only dangerous when Templeton possesses it, but is not dangerous when we possess it. It must be something that he can't pass on," continued Pollock. "I suggest identification. Suppose Templeton has seen someone and could identify him if he was in the witness-box, that would make him dangerous. At the same time he couldn't pass on his knowledge to us. Identification at second-hand isn't evidence." He paused; the others were listening intently.

"Go on," murmured the Oyster. "It's like being at a lecture."

"Now the only chance you had of seeing anyone interesting, so far as I can make out, was when you went up the path and listened to the telephone conversation."

"I didn't though," put in Templeton.

"No, but they may have thought you did. They must have found your foot-marks by the window and assumed that you saw more than you did. What about the man with the very deep voice? I suggest that he's the boss of the show, that he thinks you've spotted him, and is proportionately anxious for your removal."

"Then what about Snell and Armstrong?" said Templeton in a low voice.

"Yes, poor devils," said Chisholm. Gardiner opened an eye and observed, "You can trace trunk calls."

"An admirable sentiment," said Chisholm, "and probably one of dazzling correctness, but perhaps a little out of place."

"I mean the trunk call that Templeton overheard."

The baronet sprang up and struck Gardiner a resounding thump on the shoulder. "What a coruscating display of brains we are giving today. Of course, the trunk call that Templeton overheard; how curious I didn't think of that before."

"Very curious, indeed," said Gardiner coldly. "We must trace it at once and see where it came from."

"The telephone wire now being mended," said the Baronet, "we also can put a trunk call through. I'll get on to John Willie and ask him to do a bit of sleuthing for us in London." He went to the telephone and asked for a London call. "This is better than shooting," he went on, his excitement rising. "I can't tell you how grateful I am to you, my dear fellow, for bringing us such a capital show. While we're waiting for this call to come through, I suggest that Pollock takes the car and goes over to that hotel of yours to see what is happening there. There may be some news of nell."

It was almost dinner-time before the barrister returned. He reported that there was no word of Snell and Armstrong, and that the neighbour-hood had no suspicion that anything out of the ordinary had occurred. The fact that three young men had set out one evening and had not yet come back would have excited alarm and misgiving had the weather been stormy. But on a beautiful, calm evening, it was out of the question for anything to have happened to them. It was, therefore, assumed that they had gone to spend a couple of days with friends, and had forgotten to tell the proprietor of the hotel. Pollock had resisted the temptation to visit the farmhouse, being uncertain of the road and the lie of the ground. He had been afraid of making a false step and falling into an ambush, or else of making a fool of himself and giving away the whereabouts of Templeton.

Next morning it was decided that Chisholm should visit the hotel. It was felt that if Pollock paid two consecutive visits, somebody might become suspicious. The baronet, on the other hand, was well known in the neighbourhood, and could drop in for a drink with the landlord without arousing any comment.

Soon after he had gone, the friend whom he alluded to as John Willie telephoned from London to say that he had traced the trunk call. It had been sent from a house in the Bloomsbury district, No. 37 George Street, at present occupied by a man called Morton.

Shortly afterwards the baronet telephoned even more excitably than usual, insisting that his two friends and Templeton should immediately come across to the hotel in the luggagecarrying Ford. He met them at the door and pushed and pulled them away from the hotel towards the links.

"Come where we can't be overheard," he said in a melodramatic whisper. Then he glanced round like a stage conspirator and said "They've gone! Hopped it, hooked it, bolted, cleared out!"

"How do you know?" said Templeton.

"Oh, everybody knows," replied Chisholm.

"Then what the devil is all this secrecy about?" asked the barrister indignantly.

"Hush, my dear fellow," said Chisholm. "We don't want everybody to know that we are interested — a most elementary precaution. Apparently yesterday evening and well on into the night, lorries were going backwards and forwards taking stuff away and they were tremendously busy at the farmhouse. There were lights in all the windows and a big fire in one of the rooms. They tell me that there was a glare from one of the chimneys which could be seen distinctly for miles, and the girl went round and paid one or two little bills which they owed. You mark my words, they have cleared out. Let's go over and have a look."

They tumbled into the Ford and, under Templeton's guidance, drove as far as the junction of the cart-track and the main road. There they disembarked and advanced stealthily until the farmhouse was in full view. There was not a sign of life. No smoke was coming out of the chimneys. The blinds were heavily shuttered. The lane was deeply rutted with the marks of motor traffic.

"Let's go slow," said Templeton. "That's how it looked when I first saw it and there were plenty of people there then. In point of fact, too many, as the song says."

"I don't believe there's a soul there now," said Chisholm. "Anyway, let's chance it," and before they could stop him he was marching down the track towards the wire fence. Concealment now being useless, they followed him, Templeton cursing his impetuosity under his breath.

The gate in the fence was locked, but with the assistance of a couple of old waterproofs and a rug, they succeeded in climbing it without undue harm to their clothes. They walked round the square formed by the farmhouse and the three long barns and found that the only entrances were the side door from which the girl had emerged, the front door facing the sea and the big door of the garage which housed the lorry. All three were locked. Knocking and bell-ringing produced no result.

"Any of you qualified burglars?" said Chisholm.

The Oyster cast down his eyes and murmured, "I once was quite good with a hairpin."

"Anyone got a hairpin?" said Chisholm. "There must be some wire in the car." He went back and brought up the Ford. Gardiner, with a deprecating smile, twisted a piece of wire into mysterious shapes and unlocked the front door. "I was taught how to do that by poachers," he said by way of excuse, "when I was very young."

The farmhouse was completely empty. It had been cleared with extraordinary thoroughness. There was not a trace of any previous occupation. They went from room to room and found everywhere the same.

"Criminals on these occasions," said Chisholm, "usually leave incriminating finger-prints or bits of paper giving their name and address. At least, so I understand from novels. You mark my words, we'll find some perfectly damning evidence in a minute or two."

The barns were equally devoid of interest, except for the information that they certainly had not been used as barns. Actually they appeared to be three long workshops, but they, like the farmhouse, were quite empty. One door was found in the upper part of the farm which was locked, and Gardiner's bent wire had to be brought into action again. The room behind contained a small table and on the table lay an envelope.

"What did I tell you?" shouted Chisholm. "The criminal's one blunder. They always make one. This is a list of their names and addresses."

He stepped up to the table and said, "No, by George, it isn't! It's a letter for you, Templeton."

In dead silence Templeton opened the envelope which was addressed "George Templeton, Esq., to wait till called for." He read it aloud:

Dear Mr Templeton,

You will find something which may interest you between the double shutters of the room downstairs in which we were playing bridge that night.

Yours sincerely,

SUSAN BLAKE."

The four men looked from one to another, and then they tumbled downstairs.

"Which was the room?" said Chisholm. "Lead the way, Templeton."

They flung open each window in turn and opened the shutters. The third window, which faced north, was protected, as the note had said, by double shutters. They were made of steel, fastened by a simple latch on the inside. Between the shutters they found a large envelope, again addressed to "George Templeton, Esq., to wait till called for."

Templeton tore it open and pulled out a large photograph. It was a picture of himself, Snell and Armstrong, grouped very close together and apparently peering round a door. A black cross in ink had been drawn across the faces of the other two: his own was left untouched. Templeton could not help a slight shiver.

"What is it?" said Pollock, in a low voice. "That flash in front of the hotel," answered

Templeton. "It must have been a magnesium wire for taking a photograph. This is the result." As he spoke, a shadow passed across the window. They all looked up and saw the rat-faced man peering in. Another second and the face had vanished.

A mist had been creeping up from the sea and they suddenly realized how cold it was. A seagull cried very loud and very near, and they all started.

"Let's get out of this," said Chisholm, and the four men hurried out of the farmhouse, threw themselves over the wire fence and packed themselves into the Ford. Chisholm drove as quickly as possible back to the main road. Looking over his shoulder, Templeton could see the figure of a man running away across the fields, bending low to avoid observation.

CHAPTER VII

The Four Allies head for London

On arriving at the hotel, the four young men made a bee-line for the bar and ordered four large whiskies and soda.

"That's better," said Chisholm, as four empty glasses were simultaneously deposited on the table. "All the same, I would feel happier in London. A fine reliable body is the Metropolitan Police. Let's cut the rest of the shooting and get up to town."

Pollock nodded. "I'm inclined to agree with you."

"I feel like one of the babes in the wood up here," said Chisholm. As he spoke a stranger entered the smoking-room. He was a man of medium height, with a pleasant-looking face, with fair hair and moustache. He was perfectly dressed and had all the air of a well-to-do visitor from the South. He appeared, however, to be labouring under the stress of some strong emotion. He called for a drink, took two or three nervous steps up and down the smoking-room and then threw himself into a chair and began to run his fingers through his hair. Then he seemed to realize that his behaviour might draw attention, and he pulled himself together. "A perfect day for golf," he said politely. "How is the course playing this year?"

"Beautifully," answered Templeton. "Have you only just arrived?"

"This evening," answered the other.

"Staying for long?" inquired Templeton casually.

The other hesitated and then said, "I had intended to stay for a week but my plans are now somewhat unsettled. I think I saw your car," he added after a moment, "coming down from the direction of . . ." He waved his hand vaguely.

Templeton, on a sudden impulse, tried a shot at a venture. "Yes," he said, "we were looking at the farmhouse which was so abruptly deserted yesterday." The random shot scored a hit, for the stranger started, began to say something, and then thought better of it.

Templeton pursued the subject. "A most curious case," he said. "Why should people fly like that unless they were afraid of something?"

"Why, indeed?" said the stranger.

"They bolted like rabbits, from all accounts, and nobody seems to know where they have gone to or why they went."

"Most extraordinary," murmured the fair-haired man, and then with an obvious effort he tried to change the conversation back to golf and the condition of the links. After agreeing that the long drought had burned up the grass on a great many golf-courses, and assenting to the suggestion that the Americans are very fine players, Templeton abruptly reintroduced the subject which the stranger seemed so anxious to avoid.

"Do you know a man called Griffin?" he said.

This time he produced no impression. The stranger was on his guard. "There was a Griffin," he said smoothly, "who was up at Cambridge with me before the war. Is that the one you mean? A scientist, so far as I remember. Why do you ask?"

"Because I saw him lately up here and I thought perhaps you might have come specially to see him."

"No, I have come specially to see no one; simply to play golf."

A moment later he made some excuse, and with a polite bow left the room.

"The plot thickens," said the Oyster.

"Yes," said Chisholm. "That's a jolly suspicious sort of fellow."

"He certainly knows more than he admits," conceded Pollock, with an air of legal caution. He rang the bell. "Was that gentleman by any chance Lord Birkenhead?" he said to the waiter who answered.

"Oh, no, sir," replied the waiter. "That's Mr Alexandrovski. He comes here quite a lot." "Thank you," said Pollock.

"I never saw a man," said Chisholm, "who looked less like Lord Birkenhead."

"I know," said Pollock. "It was the first name that came into my head." He looked at his watch. "What about dining here and starting for London first thing tomorrow morning?"

They had taken their places in the dining-room before they missed Guy Gardiner, and they had finished the first course before he appeared, fingering a piece of bent wire and threading his way dreamily between the tables.

"Hallo, Oyster," said Chisholm. "What have you been up to now? We thought you had been kidnapped too."

The Oyster answered nothing, but continued to play with the piece of wire pensively; then he glanced round the room and his eye rested for a moment on Mr Alexandrovski, who was dining alone in a far corner of the room. Then he leant forward and whispered, "I couldn't resist the temptation."

"What temptation?" demanded Pollock sternly. "You've been up to some of your monkey tricks again."

"A little civility from you, Mr Pollock, please," replied Gardiner. "I happened to find a bit of wire in my hand — I assure you I have no idea how it got there — just at the moment when I was passing the bedroom door of our friend with the Russian name."

"You scoundrel," said Pollock. "How did you know the number of the room?"

"I happened to see it on the slate in the office. There seemed to be nobody about so I went in. There was a tin box in the corner so I had a look in that. Do you know what was in it?" He lowered his voice mysteriously. "Shaving brushes! Hundreds of shaving brushes!" He leant back with a detached air and devoted himself entirely to his glass, leaving the other three to make what guesses or to ask what questions they liked. "I know nothing more," he said. "You can take it or leave it."

"Why, it's obvious," said Chisholm, "the man is a traveller — a traveller in shaving brushes."

"But I thought he was the man with the house in Eaton Square," objected Templeton. "Isn't that the address he gives in the book?"

Pollock slipped out and returned in a couple of minutes. "I've been speaking to the landlord," he said. "The man does live in Eaton Square and the landlord says that he's very rich."

"Did you see anything else?" asked Chisholm, but Gardiner shook his head. "Hadn't time," he said.

Conversation flagged for a bit and Templeton, who had been sitting silent, at last asked the question that had been in his mind for several hours. "Why do you suppose they crossed out the faces in that photograph?"

There was no answer. The others looked firmly at their plates.

"There were no signs of violence," said Pollock finally, "but of course that proves nothing. There's no need to jump to conclusions until we find out a few more facts."

"There's been no word of the man who was chucked over the cliff," said Chisholm. "They don't seem to have reported his death."

"I imagine they buried him at sea," said Pollock.

"If they could bury one at sea," said Templeton, "they could bury three," and to this again the others had no answer.

The four allies arrived in London late on the following evening, and Sir Alastair Chisholm insisted on their putting up at his house in Clarges Street.

Sir Alastair was a rich young bachelor who had been left his title and his fortune a few years before. He had few relations and few responsibilities, and he stinted nothing to make himself as comfortable as possible.

They had agreed in the train that the first thing to be done, after Templeton had obtained extension of leave from his firm, was to investigate the house in Bloomsbury from which the telephone call had been sent to the farm at Gulls' Cove. The dislocated thumb, although almost well by this time, was just sufficiently painful to extract a medical certificate from a reluctant doctor that Templeton was unfit to return to his office for another week, and he returned to Clarges Street in time for lunch, to find the other three engaged in an earnest conversation. "What luck with the medico?" shouted Chisholm as soon as he saw him. "Did you succeed in bribing Harley Street?"

"I have got another week's leave," said Templeton primly, "owing to the excessively weak condition of my thumb, which makes it quite impossible for me to discharge my important duties at the offices of the Anglo-Siamese Corporation."

"Well, they'll never miss you anyway," said Chisholm. "We have been having a busy morning. We visited the Bloomsbury house."

"What was it like?" asked Templeton eagerly. "Oh, just like a house in Bloomsbury. They're all the same, but do you know who we saw? The little sportsman with the ginger hair and the face like a frightened rat, that looked in at the farm window."

"Did he see you?" said Templeton quickly. "I don't think so. He was drifting down Gower Street, and the Oyster happened to spot him in time to dive into a tobacconist's and lie low until the coast was clear. You have your uses, little man," he added patronizingly, and Gardiner blinked mildly and observed, "I wish I could say the same for you."

"We found the house all right," said Chisholm loftily ignoring the retort, "but we can't hang about at street-corners watching it all day, so we have taken furnished rooms in the house opposite, No. 34. Luckily they are empty, and the old dame who keeps the house was delighted to see our month's rent paid in advance. All we want now is a couple of packs of cards, four glasses and a barrel of beer. If we draw the curtains, we can play bridge and dummy can keep an eye on the house. We'll start immediately after lunch."

The apartments which had been so providentially vacant were on the first floor, and the window of the front room was an ideal observation post. It was fitted with heavy lace curtains through which it was easy to keep watch without being seen from the house opposite. Armed with a stock of sporting newspapers and two packs of cards, the friends settled down to their vigil. It happened that Pollock was dummy when the door of the house opposite opened and a fat, shortish man with a very white, pasty face, came shuffling out. In a moment the watchers were down in the street, lounging casually in pursuit.

The fat man, presumably the Morton who had sent the telephone call, walked very slowly, wheezing and grunting as he went. His dress was an odd mixture of shabbiness and flashiness. His collar was dirty and his shoes were down at heel, but on one hand he wore a diamond ring and it was a genuine Malacca cane with gold top that supported his considerable weight. His appearance was made especially grotesque by the brown cotton gloves which he wore.

His first port of call was the Post Office where he sent a telegram. Gardiner slipped up beside him and pretended to write a telegram on the next shelf, but Morton kept a podgy hand over the words he wrote, and he was careful to detach the telegraph form from the pad before beginning to write, so as not to leave an impression on the form below. He slipped the telegram across the counter in such a way that it was impossible to read it, and all that Gardiner could see was that the message was a long one.

The fat man made a few purchases; tea, sugar, and other groceries; bought the *Evening Standard* from a newsboy and then shuffled back to the house.

At about six o'clock he came out again and entered a public-house — re-emerging in a moment with a bottle of whisky under his arm. He did not appear again that night. Early next morning the bridge party was in full swing, but there was no sign of activity in the house opposite. It was nearly lunch time when Gardiner suddenly said, "Do you think I look like a gas inspector?"

"Well, now that you mention it," said Chisholm, "you look extremely like a gas inspector. I wonder that it never occurred to me before."

"If I had a bowler hat," said Gardiner modestly "and a little black bag, I think I would look the part. There's a hat-shop a little way down the road; I think I'll go and see."

He went out and returned with a bowler hat, a small hand-bag, a rather shabby second-hand black coat and a handful of miscellaneous tools. "I will now go and inspect the meter," he said. "Alastair must go to the Post Office in time to make certain of getting one of the telephone call-boxes.

You had better occupy it for at least ten minutes beforehand, Alastair, to make sure. Templeton can stay here and see what happens, and Charlie must stand at the door of the Post Office to signal to Alastair as soon as he sees me admitted to the house. When you get the signal, Alastair, telephone to Morton and tell him to hold the line for a trunk call from Scotland. What about that for an idea?"

"The young Napoleon," said Chisholm admiringly. "And what will happen if there is no gas meter?"

"Oh, there's bound to be a meter. All these houses have gas. Anyway, I'll take a chance on it."

He put on his newly-acquired costume, left the house and made a wide detour before approaching No. 37. With his hand on the bell he glanced round and saw Pollock standing at the entrance of the Post Office. After a pause, the door was cautiously opened by Morton, who was wearing a shabby pair of bedroom slippers and an old, torn dressing-gown.

"What is it?" he said.

"Gas Light and Coke Company," replied Gardiner briskly. "Come to see the meter." "What's wrong with the meter?" growled Morton. "There was a man here only last week to read it."

"A general survey, sir, of all meters in the Metropolitan area."

The words sounded impressive, though Gardiner had not the least idea what they meant. Fortunately Morton had no idea either, for he grudgingly opened the door and said, "Well, you must be quick about it. I'll show you the meter." He led the way along a badly-lit passage and up the first part of a flight of stairs. The meter was on a shelf at the turn of the stairs, behind a dusty strip of curtain. Gardiner pulled back the curtain and looked with what he imagined was a professional air at the instrument. Morton stood on the stairs below him and watched the proceedings. Although his eyes were mere slits in a puffy expanse of face, they were remarkably keen.

The bogus inspector pulled out a note-book and pencil and jotted down the number of the meter and made careful notes of its condition. Then he opened his little black bag and pulled out a screwdriver with which he laboriously tested all the screws. The fat man's eyes never left him. Having tested the screws, Gardiner's inventive capacity began to flag. He produced an iron bolt and tapped the meter carefully all over, listening to each of the taps with great care.

"What's that for?" said Morton suddenly.

"That's the way to tell if any of the dials inside have got loose," replied Gardiner at random.

"Dials inside! What does that mean?" Gardiner was beginning to feel extremely hot and embarrassed when, at that moment, the telephone bell rang. "Thank God," he murmured under his breath.

Morton went down two steps and looked again at the inspector; that official was busy tapping away at the meter as if his life depended on it. The bell went on ringing and Morton, after another hesitation on the stair, finally made up his mind and shuffled with as much speed as he could into the room on the left-hand side of the passage, closing the door of the room carefully behind him.

As soon as Gardiner heard the gruff, wheezy voice answering the telephone, he made a lightning dash upstairs, carefully keeping to the side of the house that was on the right-hand side of the front door to lessen the chance of Morton hearing his footsteps. He gently entered a room, found all the furniture covered with dust-sheets, backed out again and tried another. It was clearly the fat man's bedroom. Gardiner swept a comprehensive glance round the disordered and untidy room, snatched a couple of envelopes from the floor, a blotting pad from a little table in the corner, and shot back to the meter.

He packed his tools and went downstairs again. Pausing in front of the door of the room containing the telephone, he could hear the heavy voice grumbling away. He boldly opened the door and began to say, "Your meter is all right, sir," but the fat man interrupted and shouted at him, "Go to hell out of here!" Gardiner promptly withdrew, but not before he had seen a table covered with dozens of shaving brushes of different sizes.

After another long detour through Bloomsbury, in order to make certain that he was not being followed, he returned to No. 34 to report the results of his visit.

They first studied the two envelopes; one bore the post-mark of Winchester while the other came from Warsaw. The blotting-paper they held up to a mirror in the approved style of detective stories, but could identify nothing of it except a few meaningless fragments and the letters "hester."

"That's Winchester again," said Pollock sagely. "That must have been when he answered the letter. We must investigate Winchester."

About half an hour after the return of the gas inspector events began to move once again in No. 37. The door was suddenly thrown open and Morton, Still in his bedroom slippers, came waddling as fast as his figure would allow him into the street. He looked up and down and then set off towards the Tottenham Court Road. The amateur detectives had hardly reached the street when he drove up again in a taxi and hurried back into the house.

Chisholm raced off to get another taxi. While he was gone, Morton came out and down the steps with a large tin box under his arm, squeezed himself into the cab and was driven off at a good rate.

A moment later, another taxi came tearing along the road, with Chisholm's face at the window. There was not a second to be lost and Templeton simply pointed to the cab in front which was disappearing round the corner and shouted, "Go ahead."

Half an hour later the baronet returned, in an extremely bad temper. He marched up and down the furnished sitting-room, cursing himself for being a fool and the fat man for being a knave. Judicious questioning and a lot of sympathy finally got the story out of him.

"I was properly had for a mug," he said. "That fat brute got out of the cab at Tottenham Court Road tube station. He put the big box under his arm, staggered into the station and bought a ticket to the Bank. Of course I followed. He waddled into the lift without a glance round and I thought everything was all right. I didn't dare to get too close to him because I didn't want to be spotted, in case he knew anything. We were the first people in the lift and both the doors were open. Then a few other people came in, and the lift attendant pulled the switch that shuts the door on the far side. As soon as he pulled the switch, what does the old brute do but jump like a two-year-old out of the lift, just before the gate shut behind him. Then the other gate shut and the lift went down, and there I was, going off to the Bank, while Morton or whatever his name is, was left up above. He must have found it difficult to walk for laughing.

"Of course I came up in the next lift, but by that time he might have been in Timbuctoo for all I knew. He's not half such a fool as he looks."

They cut through the pack of cards to decide who should remain on guard and the lot fell on Templeton. The other three departed for the Berkeley Hotel, via Clarges Street.

CHAPTER VIII

Inspector Roberts of Scotland Yard

Next morning Templeton was surprised to find a letter waiting for him at Chisholm's house, requesting his immediate attendance at Scotland Yard. He was on the point of starting when Pollock looked up from his breakfast plate and said: "By the way, what are you going to tell them about Morton? I think you ought to tell them everything else, but that's our own pet discovery. I don't think there's any need to let them into that."

"I don't think there's any need to let them into anything," said Chisholm. "We shall have far more fun without them."

"It's not a question of fun," said Pollock. "Templeton certainly ought to tell them all the facts, but I don't think it's absolutely necessary to tell them how we followed up one of the facts."

Templeton agreed, and he omitted the Morton episode from the long story which he had to tell Inspector Roberts of Scotland Yard. It was the same story that he had told the Chief Constable of Inverness. Inspector Roberts listened without comment until the story was finished, and then he said:

"There's no doubt that your two friends have disappeared. The Home Office have been speaking to us about Mr Snell and neither Mr Armstrong's firm nor his family have heard from him for nearly a week."

He opened a file which lay beside him and began to turn over a lot of loose pages. "Does the name Li Chu convey anything to you, Mr Templeton?"

"Nothing whatever," said Templeton. "Or Abd-el-Rahman?"

Templeton shook his head again. "Or Alexandrovski?"

"Oh, yes, I met him at the hotel up in Scotland, and now that I come to think of it I saw the name Li Chu on the hotel register when I was up there."

"Yes, this is a copy of the register," said Inspector Roberts.

Templeton told him briefly of his meeting with Alexandrovski.

"Now this man Griffin," went on the official. "We have looked him up but we can't trace what his movements were after he left the Army."

Templeton stared at him in surprise. "What do you mean when you say you have looked him up? How did you know anything about him? And if it comes to that, how did you get a copy of the hotel register?"

It was the Inspector's turn to stare. "You told all this to the Chief Constable in Inverness?"

"Yes, but it went in at one of the old donkey's ears and out at the other."

"Some of it seems to have stuck," said the Inspectr with a laugh. "Anyway, he seems to have remembered the name Griffin. You can't throw any light on his movements, I suppose?"

"I never saw him from the time I left Cambridge till the time I met him on the road looking for the bomb."

Next day Templeton was surprised to receive another summons to Scotland Yard. He was again shown into Inspector Roberts' room and there, to his astonishment, he found the Inspector and the small man with the red hair who looked like a rat.

"By Jove, sir," he exclaimed excitedly. "So you've got him."

"Got who?" asked the Inspector, rather taken aback at this abrupt greeting.

"This sportsman with the funny face," said Templeton.

Roberts laughed, and the other man smiled for a moment.

"Allow me to introduce you," said Roberts. "This is Inspector Fraser of the Inverness police."

Templeton began to stammer something, but the Scotsman cut him short by holding out his hand and saying, "Glad to meet you in more pleasant circumstances, Mr Templeton."

Templeton shook his hand warmly and then said: "So that was why the policeman appeared in the nick of time at the Post Office."

"That was it," said Inspector Fraser dryly. "Did you think it was a coincidence?"

"I thought it was the hand of God," replied Templeton simply. "It was too good to be true." "Now, Mr Templeton," said Roberts, "we have got a bone to pick with you. When you told me that long story yesterday you didn't say anything about a Mr Morton of 37 George Street, Bloomsbury."

"So you spotted him too," said Templeton. "Well done."

Fraser snorted. "I like that from an amateur," he said; and Roberts continued: "The idea had occurred to us, Mr Templeton, surprising though it may appear, and we had Mr Morton's house under observation until you and your friends butted in and so effectively gave the show away."

"I am extremely sorry," began Templeton; but the official waved his apologies aside. "What's done can't be undone. The important thing is that it should not happen again. Have you got any more little surprises up your sleeve?"

The two detectives listened with close attention to the story of the invasion of 37 George Street, and the subsequent flight of the fat man.

At the end Roberts said, "Now, Mr Templeton, this amateur detective business must stop, at any rate your independent — er — investigations. We want you to keep an eye open for Griffin and this girl, Susan Blake. You are the only person who seems to know them by sight. If you like to have your friends in to help you, that's your own affair, but I must impress upon you that we must work together, and that you must tell either Fraser or myself exactly what you are doing or what you propose to do. On those terms I shall be very glad to have your cooperation."

"It would never have happened," said Templeton, "if I hadn't got the impression that the Inverness police were a set of——" He broke off in confusion, remembering that Fraser was a member of that body, and it was Fraser who completed his sentence. "A set of damned idiots. Well, well, perhaps we are not so silly as we appear."

"But that Chief Constable of yours," protested Templeton. "He didn't listen to a word I said, and didn't take any interest in anything except fishing."

"All the same, we got you out of a pretty nasty hole," said Fraser with a twinkle.

"Why didn't you tell me you were taking the whole thing up?" said Templeton.

Fraser laughed. "Because you made such a capital decoy, Mr Templeton. If you had known you were being protected, you would not have behaved in such a natural way, you would not have looked half so scared," he added with a touch of friendly malice. He looked at his watch. "It's time I was off, Roberts," he said. "One more question," said the young man. "Have you searched Morton's house?"

"As soon as we heard that he had bolted," answered Roberts. "We got a search warrant and went up, but we were too late; the house was on fire and was blazing merrily by the time we arrived. They seem to be a fairly resourceful set of gentlemen."

The Scottish detective had slipped away and Templeton, feeling that the interview was at an end, took up his hat and made for the door. With his hand on the door-knob he turned to Roberts and said: "What is it all about, Inspector? What's at the bottom of it all?" The official considered for a moment and then said, "I doubt if I know more than you do. I think we both of us know that this gang of people have got a weapon of some sort which they are selling to anyone with the money to buy it. It's quite certain that the weapon, whatever it is, has not yet been used, at any rate on a large scale, or we would have heard of it. But I'll tell you a funny thing: both Glasgow and Birmingham tell me that lately there has been a distinct falling off in the demand for munitions from what you might call unauthorized sources. By that I mean private citizens, not governments. The armament firms do a certain amount of trade with individuals as well as with governments. On the other hand, there is no doubt that there is a lot of quiet excitement among political exiles in England. Alexandrovski, for instance, is extremely busy."

"Who is Alexandrovski?" put in Templeton. "Isn't he an Englishman?"

"No. He was at school in England and speaks perfect English. But he's a Russian. He is one of the leaders of the Anti-Bolshevik Russians over here. He has also asked for police protection, which is rather significant."

"Significant of what?" asked Templeton.

"Well, those Russian exiles don't cut very much ice as a rule, and the Bolsheviks pay very little attention to them. They do more talking than anything else, but during the last few weeks, for the first time since 1918, Alexandrovski is afraid that he may be attacked. That looks as if he was on to something big and somebody else knew about it. He's rather afraid of the same fate as that Irishman up in Scotland."

"The Irishman! Do you know who he was?"

"No," said the Inspector. "But I have little doubt that he was a Republican trying to upset the Free State and that the men who shot him were practically official messengers. But of course, all this is outside our province in this particular affair. We're trying to trace two missing men. So far there's no question of anything else."

"A last question," said Templeton again. "How did Morton spot that we were after him?"

"He rang up the Gas Company," said the Inspector, "to ask if they really had sent a man round to look at his meter."

CHAPTER IX

The Mysterious Mr Morton

"There's one thing I don't understand," said Charles Pollock, helping himself to marmalade at Sir Alastair Chisholm's breakfast table.

"There's a great deal more than one thing you don't understand," said Chisholm, who was reading *The Times* with his feet on the mantelpiece.

"It's a rather disquieting thought," went on Pollock, ignoring his retort, "if not for us, at any rate for our newly-found friend and brother, Mr George Templeton of the Anglo-Siamese Trading Corporation."

"What's that about me?" said Templeton. "I have had a disquieting thought about you," said the barrister. "Why are you still alive?"

"What a pleasant fellow he is at the breakfast-table," murmured Gardiner to himself. Pollock proceeded, "You don't see what I mean."

"Oh yes, we do, thanks," said Chisholm. "Write it down and we will look at it later."

"Let me recall to you the circumstances in which we first made the acquaintance of our trusty friend," went on the indomitable Pollock.

"No, thanks," said Gardiner.

"He was at that moment pretty well on the run, and it was only my providential appearance . . ."

"*Our* providential appearance," said Chisholm. "Very well," said Pollock, "our providential appearance, if you like, though I fancy it was my presence rather than yours that scared off the desperadoes."

"It was your face," said the Oyster. "It reminded them too much of Dartmoor."

"At any rate, he was on the run," said Pollock. "He's apparently no longer on the run. No one fires pistols at him through the window, nor are poisoned snakes or chocolates containing prussic acid sent him by every post. These, I believe, are the usual methods of getting rid of people that one doesn't like. He's no longer threatened with abduction in broad daylight, nor does he receive letters asking him to proceed at once to Limehouse to hear of something to his advantage."

"You're quite right," said Chisholm, putting down *The Times*. "I never thought of that."

"I did," said Templeton rather grimly. "I found the change a distinct relief."

"It seems to me," went on Pollock, "that there are two reasons for their letting you alone — either because they are on the run themselves and are too busy to do anything else except retreat, or else you are no longer dangerous to them."

"And what about the third reason?" said Gardiner, looking up.

"I didn't say there were three reasons. I only said there were two."

"But the third reason is even more likely to be the true one. It is that they know I am always at George Templeton's side." Gardiner looked proudly round and Chisholm threw a bedroom slipper at him.

"Now, let me recapitulate the whole singular series of events," said Pollock.

"No, thanks," said Gardiner, while Chisholm picked up the poker and roared at the barrister, "Shut up, you idiot."

"Very well," said the barrister cheerfully. "I will not recapitulate, but I will ask you a question. What is this gang of people frightened of? What is it that scares them stiff?"

"Me," said the Oyster modestly.

"We come back to where we were at the beginning," said Pollock. "We can't find out what crime they have committed; that is, what crime did they commit before they abducted your friends, Snell and Armstrong. That is the first time, so far as I can make out, that they have put themselves outside the law, because it is no crime in this country to manufacture weapons. I'm a little hazy on the point, but I think that all that's necessary is a licence to export them, which can be easily got. Why, then, should law-abiding citizens get into such a panic that they commit two very serious crimes and draw the whole attention of the police on them. The answer is obvious," he went on. "Because they are afraid of something even more than they are afraid of the police. What, then, is that something?"

"Stop asking silly questions," said Chisholm, "and tell us what you mean."

"I am only asking questions," said Pollock in an aggrieved tone, "in order to show you that you can't answer them and I can. If we assume that they have got hold of a secret weapon and are selling it, as the Inspector told Templeton, to revolutionaries and sportsmen of that sort, it follows that they must be extremely unpopular with the people on whom the weapon is going to be used by the revolutionaries. Take the case of the Irishman, for instance. Assume that he was sent by the Republic to get the weapon, and assume that the two men who shot him were Free Staters. It's only one step from shooting the messenger who is going to get the weapon, to shooting the people who are actually producing the weapon itself. In fact, when you come to think of it, it's a great deal more effective. Why hasn't it been done before? All right, I'll tell you," he went on hastily, as Chisholm rose with a threatening air. "Because they have been so jolly clever at hiding themselves, and until George Templeton stumbled on them, hardly anyone had any idea of their identity. In other words, if Alexandrovski is an anti-Bolshevik, then our friends are afraid of the Bolshies. If they want to sell to the Republicans, they have got to look out for the Free Staters.

"I have no doubt that Moorish fellow we saw was one of those tribes that are always revolting against Spain or France or Italy, in which case they will have to look out for reprisals from old Mussolini. You see what I mean?"

"We do," said Chisholm. "At least I do, and I always did say that for brains, Charles Pollock, you are hard to beat."

Templeton listened keenly to this exposition. At the end he said, "The logical conclusion, then, is that we're on the same side as a lot of queer people, Bolshies."

"Damn it," exclaimed Chisholm energetically. "I won't be on the same side as Bolshies. I'd sooner be on the other side. I'd sooner drop the whole game. I'd sooner — I'd sooner ——" He choked with indignation.

"We needn't actively help them," said Pollock soothingly.

"I should jolly well think not," was the emphatic reply. "If there's any question of helping those blackguards, you can count me out of the whole thing. And Lord knows," he added sadly, "I'm enjoying it as much as I've enjoyed anything in my life."

"It's rather complicated," said Pollock thoughtfully. "We haven't much to go on. There's the identification of the girl, the identification of Griffin, and the letter with the Winchester postmark which the Oyster found chez M. Morton in George Street."

"Look here," said Chisholm, "you fellows stay in town and look for Griffin and the girl, while I go down to Winchester and have a look round and see what I can see."

"It's all rather vague," commented Pollock, "but I think it's about all we can do."

"I'll start at once," said the impulsive baronet, seizing his coat and motoring gloves.

"Half a minute," shouted Templeton. "Don't be in such a hurry. What are you going to do when you get to Winchester?"

"Do some sleuthing. I'll wire to you results," and Chisholm rushed out. They leant out of the window and shouted to him as he sprang into his big car which was standing in front of the door. Chisholm only looked up, grinned, and waved his hand. Next moment there was the roar of the engines and the car glided away, accelerated rapidly and shot round the corner.

Pollock shook his head. "Alastair's such an impulsive chap," he said. "Lord only knows what he'll do when he gets to Winchester. Let's hope he finds nothing. Now, what are we going to do?"

"We can't really do very much till the police want us," said Templeton. "We might try and dig up news of Griffin's whereabouts. I'll try and get hold of one or two contemporaries of mine at Cambridge."

For the next forty-eight hours there was no new development, except the arrival of an incoherent Marconigram from Chisholm. Templeton's efforts to get on Griffin's track were a failure. The young men grew a little bored. Each line of investigation taken up by the police ended in a dead blank. The description of Morton had been circulated, but no information had been gained of any value.

Another line of inquiry was the tracing of the lorry loads from the farm in Scotland, such as Templeton had seen on the occasion of his first meeting with Griffin. The loads had consisted mainly of wooden boxes, which had been dispatched by rail from the station of Keith, in Aberdeenshire, to Euston, to lie there in the name of Morton until called for, and officials in the goods office at Euston were perfectly familiar with Morton's appearance.

The fat man used to call for the boxes with a lorry and drive off to some unknown destination. The police were busy trying to trace the man who had driven the lorry for him, but so far had had no success.

The man arrested in Inverness for being in unlawful possession of fire-arms turned out to be well known to the police of the East End of London. He had served several terms of imprisonment for robbery with violence. The pistol in his possession was traced to a gunsmith in Shaftesbury Avenue, and it was found to have been sold to Griffin some months before. The man, whose name was supposed to be Harry Wells, refused to give any information about his employers. He had been hired at the house of a friend of his by Morton, and he had clearly been well paid, for a considerable sum of money was found upon him. He denied all knowledge of Snell or Armstrong, and kept on simply repeating that he had been employed to look after a motor-lorry. That was his sole job. The pistol had been given to him, he said, because of an alarm of burglars.

Inspector Fraser paid a visit to the East End of London and had a long conversation with the chief inspector of one of the East London police stations. As a result of this conversation, inquiries were made which resulted in the information that Harry Wells had not been seen for some months in the neighbourhood, but that a usual haunt of his had been a lodging-house in a side lane off the Commercial Road, East.

A rubber of bridge was in progress at Clarges Street when Inspector Fraser was ushered in and announced that he required the attendance of two of the four friends that night. The lodging-house was to be raided and identification of Morton might be necessary. "I would like Mr Templeton and you two gentlemen to come," said Fraser. "If it's quite convenient to you, I'll expect you at six sharp at Scotland Yard. Ask for Inspector Roberts."

That evening on the way down to the East End, Roberts cautioned the young men against taking any action of any sort during the raid. "I want you to remember," he said, "that you are coming down simply to identify a man. If there is a rough house you'll have to leave it to us.

They got off the omnibus at Aldgate and walked the rest of the distance. About half a mile down the Commercial Road they were overtaken by a big man in a soft hat and overcoat, who said to Roberts in a low tone as he passed, "Everything is ready, sir." They followed him to a small turning, down which he plunged without hesitation. A man who had been leaning in a shadowy corner against the wall, came forward.

"All ready, Williams?" said Roberts. "Yes, sir," said the other.

"Well, then, let her rip!"

The man addressed as Williams turned and waved his arm down an alley. The next moment there was a silent rush of big men in soft hats and overcoats towards the fifth house down the lane.

The door was locked and there was a moment's delay. Sounds of commotion and disturbance, however, showed that an entry had been forced at some other point, and then the front door was opened from the inside. The little knot of men who were listening in the street heard shouts, then an outburst of swearing and cursing, the sound of furniture being overturned and then complete silence.

A head came out of one of the upstairs windows and a voice said, "It's all right, sir. Everything is quiet."

"Come on," said Roberts; and he led the way, followed by Fraser and his unofficial allies.

So swiftly and efficiently had the raid been carried out that it was all over before the neighbours realized what had happened. The street remained deserted.

Upstairs the sulky proprietor of the lodging-house was protesting to the sergeant his complete innocence of any and every crime in the calendar. Half a dozen squalid lodgers were lined up in another room.

At first the proprietor denied all knowledge of anyone, but his tone changed quickly when Roberts said in a quiet voice, "I want this man Morton on a serious charge; it may turn out to be a murder charge."

The lodging-house keeper collapsed at the word "murder," and became voluble with information. Two days ago a big, fat man whom he knew by the name of Freeman came to him for a room. He had known him before but knew nothing of his life or occupation; indeed, his stock of information boiled down to the fact that his lodger paid well and in advance. He had gone out that morning and had not yet returned.

A minute and expert search of the room occupied by the wanted man revealed hardly anything. There was a mark in the dust in one corner which might have corresponded to the outline of the box which Morton had taken under his arm in his flight from George Street. The proprietor said that he distinctly remembered the man coming with a box, but he could not say when he had removed it.

The only other sign of occupation was a rolled-up ball of paper which seemed to have been used for cleaning a plate after some sort of meal. It was a page from a catalogue of a dealer in shaving brushes.

When the search had concluded the police were withdrawn, with the exception of a couple of men who were left to watch for Morton's return, and the party returned to the local police station and thence to Scotland Yard.

"That was bad luck," said Roberts, "missing him as closely as that. It seems to me we're having a lot of bad luck."

"I'm not quite so sure about the luck," said Fraser. "They're pretty good at covering their tracks, these people."

"I don't see how Morton could have known we were going to raid the place," said Roberts. "Suppose he heard from Griffin or someone," said Fraser, "that Wells had been taken at Inverness. He would know that something was up and he would soon put two and two together. He was living in the house in which he had hired Wells, so he puts his box under his arm and beats it. He won't go back. Let's try the catalogue." Next morning Roberts and Fraser visited the offices of Messrs. Tyler & Dempster, manufacturers of shaving brushes, Queen Victoria Street. The manager opened his sales book to the detectives and they found that on several occasions quantities of a hundred brushes at a time had been dispatched to Alexandrovski, at his Eaton Square address.

The manager very quickly pointed out those of his customers who were not in the trade and to whom, therefore, trade discount was not given. The Russian, of course, was one of those. Another was a William Smithson, 14 Vauxhall Bridge Road, and the third was a G. Lawrence, the High Street, Acton.

"These are the only three private customers who bought quantities of a hundred or more at a time," said the manager.

Both Smithson and Lawrence proved on investigation to be small stationers' shops which served as "accommodation addresses." In each case the proprietor told the detectives that parcels used to come at fairly long intervals, and had been called for by a pasty-faced, fat man in a taxi.

The detectives brought the result of those investigations round to Clarges Street. This time they had come to pick up Gardiner.

"We want your help, Mr Gardiner," said Roberts. "We are going round to Mr Alexandrovski's house to ask him point blank what he wants with shaving brushes. It was you who saw them in his room, I understand?"

"That makes it rather awkward," said Gardiner. "How am I to explain how I saw them. I can't very well tell him that I picked the lock of his door."

"I don't suppose you'll be asked to say anything, as a matter of fact," said Roberts, "but you had better think up some story if you don't like to admit yourself an experienced burglar."

They drove round to Eaton Square and found the Russian at home. The Inspector went straight to the point.

"Why all those shaving brushes, sir?" he said. The Russian raised his eyebrows elegantly. "I am not sure that I follow the question."

"Why do you keep all those shaving brushes in that box?" repeated the Inspector bluntly.

"In what box?"

"The box you took up to Scotland."

The Russian gazed steadily at the inspector, and then looked from him to Fraser and then to Gardiner. The two detectives returned his look with equal steadiness, but Gardiner modestly lowered his eyes and stared at the carpet.

"If I tell you," said the Russian, "will you answer a question?"

"I don't promise," said Roberts.

The Russian laughed and then waved to the easy chairs. "Sit down," he said, "help yourselves to a drink." He brought out a decanter and glasses. "You may have heard," he went on, "that I am one of our National Committee for the relief of Russian exiles. We collect what money we can and use it as best we can. Sometimes it is food we send them, sometimes it is clothes, sometimes it is money for a ticket to America, sometimes it is money for a passport, sometimes it is medicine. Yesterday it was quinine for those of my unfortunate compatriots who are suffering from malaria in the Balkan Peninsula. Today it is shaving brushes." He looked again steadily at Inspector Roberts.

"Why is there such a demand for shaving-brushes?" put in Fraser, and the Russian turned to face him.

He waved a beautifully-manicured hand and said, "It is self-respect, my dear Inspector. You must realize that many thousands of these exiles were once rich men, barons, counts, princes, dukes, even Grand Dukes, accustomed to a life of comfort and ease and luxury. Can you blame them if they want to recover a little of their self-respect by looking after their appearance. A Russian only neglects his appearance when he is in despair. We do not yet despair. Hence the shaving-brushes." He waved his hand again. "Foolish, perhaps — but rather magnificent."

There was dead silence and then Alexandrovski said lightly, "And now for my question. How did you know I had the shaving-brushes in my box?"

Gardiner looked up and fixed his round blue eyes on Alexandrovski. "Because I burgled your room, sir. It's a trick I learnt when I was young."

The Russian stood up. "Now that we have answered each other's questions satisfactorily, is there anything further I can do for you?" He ushered his visitors to the door with a graceful ease that was evidence of long familiarity with the world and its ways.

The two inspectors and Gardiner walked in silence until they were out of earshot, and then Roberts turned to Fraser and said, "What an infernal lie."

"Yes," said Fraser, "but rather a plausible one."

CHAPTER X

Sir Alastair Sails to Madeira

Excitement carried Sir Alastair Chisholm several miles before he quietened down and reflected that he was en route for Winchester at a considerable speed without the slightest idea of what he was to look for when he arrived. The perplexity caused by this reflection did not last long. Chisholm was the type that does not worry very much about anything and certainly does not worry for more than a minute at a time.

"Oh well, something will turn up," he said to himself, accelerating to sixty-five miles an hour as he left London behind and came out onto a magnificent stretch of concrete road. He achieved the fifty or sixty miles to Winchester uneventfully for himself, though by no means uneventfully for pedestrians, chickens and other cars. On arriving he drove to the George, put up the car, reserved a room and ordered a drink. When the drink came he sat down in the hotel lounge to consider the situation. The problem was easy. He had to find something suspicious, something to do with bombs. So far, so good. The next question was how to set about it. He stared at the ceiling, he stared at the floor, and he stared at the walls. None of these provided inspiration. He took his hat and went for a walk down the picturesque old High Street, back again up to the top of the High Street, and then to the hotel for lunch. Inspiration was completely lacking. "Well, well," he said to himself placidly. "Something will turn up," and he attacked his lunch with great gusto.

After lunch, the young man took his car and drove slowly round the town wondering what to do next. He stopped in the Cathedral Close and, in search of inspiration, went into the Cathedral and strolled about in the cool shadows. But the vaulted nave and the tomb of William of Wykeham were as unhelpful as the lounge of the hotel. He went out into the sunlight and walked slowly back to his car. Then he stopped. A small, poorly-dressed man was taking a remarkable interest in his car. It is true that it was of striking appearance. A six-cylinder two-seater, painted cream-white with scarlet wheels and mud-guards, is certain to be noticed. But this man was walking round it, staring at it with more than casual interest. Then he turned round and took to his heels and fairly bolted out of the Close. Chisholm got a very strong impression that this sudden retreat was not due to his own approach but to something peculiar in the car. But the baronet had never been the man to analyse impressions or weigh up motives or balance various courses of action. The little man was scuttling away. Chisholm dashed in pursuit. His long legs and excellent training helped him to overhaul his quarry rapidly. But what the little man lacked in speed, he made up in local knowledge and a few dexterous turns and twists in the narrow streets outside the wall of the Close enabled him to get clean away. Chisholm returned to the car, partly disappointed at his failure and partly elated at the proof of his wisdom in coming to Winchester and the truth of his prediction that something would happen.

He opened the cut-out of his engine in order to make the maximum amount of noise and for the next two hours he rent the air of the quiet old, historical, scholastic and ecclesiastical city with the explosions of his cylinders, for which he was duly summoned by the Winchester police force. "If someone is interested in the car," he thought, "I'll give them every chance of seeing it."

When he was tired of driving, he tried a new line. He went round the hotels asking if any Russians were at present among the visitors. The sight of his card, his good looks and his charming manners made the various bureau clerks and managers give him the required information. His delight and triumph were unbounded when he found the name Alexandrovski amongst the visitors who had in the past patronized the Black Swan. By the time he returned to the George in time for a cocktail before dinner, Chisholm felt that he was rapidly unravelling the mystery which had baffled not only his two brainy friends, Pollock and Gardiner, but the full force and talent of Scotland Yard itself.

While he was sipping his dry Martini with the utmost satisfaction, the hall-porter came across the lounge to him.

"There's a lady to see you, my lord," he said deferentially.

"A lady?" Chisholm started up. "It must be a mistake. Chisholm's my name. Not Lord anything."

"I beg your pardon, sir, but Sir Alast Chisholm."

"Alastair — not Alast."

"I beg your pardon, sir, but it's Sir Alastair Chisholm that she asked for."

"All right," said the baronet cheerfully, straightening his tie. "Show her in and bring a couple more of these Martinis — one dry and one sweet."

The porter bowed and the next moment was ushering an odd-looking pair across the room. In front was a girl, small, pretty, with black hair and eyebrows and a dark olive complexion. She was neatly but shabbily dressed. Her unfashionably long skirt had been darned at least once and not too skilfully. Black cotton stockings and low-heeled, cheap shoes did not impress the young man very favourably, nor did the obvious mend in a finger of her black kid gloves. But in spite of it, she was undeniably pretty in a queer, Eastern sort of way. And yet it wasn't exactly Eastern. Chisholm could not place it.

Behind her was a man, also dressed very poorly. His face was very pale and lined with premature wrinkles. One sleeve of his shabby grey coat was empty. He leant heavily on a stick and limped. The girl went straight up to the young man and looked up at him appealingly. "Sir Alastair," she said with a distinct foreign accent. He bowed. "This is my brother," she went on nervously. "He does not speak English." Both men bowed and Chisholm said awkwardly "Er — do sit down — Miss — er," but she did not help him out.

"Sir Alastair," she leant forward and clasped her gloved hands together. "You go round the hotels this evening, asking are there any Russians. Will you, can you tell me why you do that?"

Chisholm was rather taken aback and he temporized. "Why do you ask, Miss — er?" There was a short silence during which the waiter arrived with the drinks. The girl refused hers, but her brother drank it eagerly. Then she sighed deeply and said, "Sir Alastair, I can trust you. I can see it in your face. I will tell you why I ask. We are Russians, the most unhappy of people. Now you know why I come to you."

"Er — not quite," murmured Chisholm.

"You seek Russians. We are Russians. Is it for us you seek? Have you brought us news? That is all?"

The young man was embarrassed. He cleared his throat once or twice and at last replied vaguely, "It's a long story."

"Then listen while I tell you mine."

He was immensely relieved and smiled in so friendly a way that the girl also brightened.

"Our story, it is sad. But it is the common lot of Russians today; I do not complain. But I will not bore you with the tale. Like the rest of us, we lost home and money, father and mother and friends. We lived in Warsaw, then in Paris. Then in London. All our money was gone. I sold my jewels. A week ago I had two diamonds left. That was all. I came here to meet a man who was to buy them. I gave them to him. He goes away. He promises to send me the money. No money comes. We live here, almost starving. Then he writes, 'Come to Cherbourg. I will hand over the money.' But we have no money to go to Cherbourg. We have nothing. Then we hear that you are asking for Russians. But you have no news of my diamonds." She looked at him with tears in her eyes.

Chisholm was deeply affected by her tale and the beauty of the teller. "Damned Bolsheviks," he muttered savagely, and then he spoke aloud. "Well, that's easily settled," he said, pulling out his pocket-book. "Let me advance you money for your passage to Cherbourg."

"You are too kind," she murmured. "But it is too late. I must go to London. Mr Templeton . . ."

"Templeton!" exclaimed Chisholm. Do you know him?"

Her large eyes opened wide. "Georges Templeton is an old friend and benefactor. He writes to me today that he wants my help. He is mixed up with Russians and I must go at once to London. I know all the Bolshevik spies in England and I hasten to help Georges."

"By Jove!" said Chisholm enthusiastically. "Then we're on the same side. Waiter, two more Martinis."

At this order the eyes of the man who knew no English sparkled in an odd way.

"Look here," went on the young man, lowering his voice prudently. "Templeton and I are working together on this thing. So it'll be perfectly all right for you to run across to Cherbourg. . . ."

She stiffened. "I must go to Georges. He has sent for me. He is my friend."

"Well, you're a loyal friend and no mistake," said Chisholm warmly.

"We Russians have little left but loyalty," she answered sadly. "I would sooner keep faith with a friend than have the three thousand pounds."

Chisholm was startled. "Three thousand. Phew! Look here, Miss — er — do you trust me enough to let me go to Cherbourg and fetch your money?"

She sat up with clasped hands and her eyes shone with gratitude. "Oh, Sir Alastair . . ."

He cut her short. "That's all right then. I can get a boat from somewhere, I suppose."

"From Southampton. It leaves tonight. It's a German liner but calls at Cherbourg. I know, as I had meant to go on it. You've just time." She was again beginning a flow of grateful thanks and was again cut short. The impulsive baronet shouted for his bill, rushed upstairs for his bag, rushed down again bag in hand, threw down a fiver at the bureau and exclaimed, "I'll be back tomorrow. I'll get the change then," and dashed out to his car. He found the girl already seated in it and the one-armed Russian clambering into the dickey.

"We must see you off," she exclaimed. "I know exactly where the boat is lying. We must hurry."

During the journey to Southampton, which they did in remarkably quick time, the girl explained minutely to Chisholm exactly where to go and what to do in Cherbourg. He insisted on her taking a five-pound note for the journey back and for arranging for the garage of his car.

It was past eight o'clock when they drew up on a quay just as a large liner was being cast off. Waving his hand to the girl, Chisholm jumped from the car and raced up the gangway just in time. The next moment the great ship began to move.

He leaned over the side and waved till a warehouse came between him and the car. Then he turned to the official who was waiting to discuss the question of fares and berths with him. He pulled out his pocket-book, handed it to the official, and said, "First single to the first stop, captain, and where's the bar?" The smiling individual in dark blue and gold buttons pointed out the bar and returned in a few minutes with the pocket-book, somewhat lightened, and a first-class ticket to Madeira.

On the quay the white-faced Russian was restoring his missing arm to its proper place in his sleeve and observing respectfully, "Well, you are a wonder, Miss."

CHAPTER XI

The Meeting with Susan Blake

While Templeton, Gardiner and Pollock were reading an immensely long Marconigram of almost apoplectically violent language (within the limits of the rules of the Marconi service) in which Chisholm described how he had been lured into a voyage to Madeira and back, a strange visitor was announced. A dark, middle-aged man, who gave his name as Clark and who spoke with a foreign accent, asked for the pleasure of an interview with Templeton. He was shown into the dining-room, where the three friends were just finishing lunch. He had two fingers missing from his left hand, and there was an indefinably unpleasant air about him. The young men instinctively took a dislike to him.

He had the confident, rather threatening manner of the unchallenged bully. Although perfectly polite and courteous, he gave the distinct impression that he was not accustomed to being trifled with, thwarted or treated in anything but the most respectful manner.

The stranger went straight to the point of his visit. "I have the pleasure to speak to Mr Templeton?" he asked, looking from one to the other, and George bowed. "I visited your flat," he went on, "and they told me you were staying here. It is about the mysterious business in Scotland." He paused, obviously expecting some kind of an answer. None being forthcoming, he went on, "I heard about you from my good friend, Mr Alexandrovski, or rather owing to Mr Alexandrovski, for I cannot actually say that I got the information from him."

Again there was no response. "I was wondering," he said, "whether you could tell me who was the owner of that place. I was wondering whether he was an old friend of mine, for whom I have been searching for some time."

The pause after this remark was so prolonged that Gardiner felt he ought to say something, and he said, gently, "Indeed."

"I have some specially good news for him," proceeded Mr Clark. "I was appointed executor in the will of a mutual friend of ours who died a couple of years ago, leaving his property almost entirely to my friend. Since then I have spent much time in trying to trace his whereabouts, so that I could hand over the money.

It was only recently that I received information which led me to think that my old friend might be the owner of that farm."

"What did your friend look like?" said Templeton.

Mr Clark shrugged his shoulders. "It is almost impossible for me to say, it is so long since I saw him. Perhaps you could describe him to me and tell me where he is likely to be found?"

"Doesn't your friend Alexandrovski know?" put in Pollock.

"Unfortunately, no. I need hardly say that any reliable information that I can get will be handsomely paid for. Very handsomely indeed," he added.

Templeton got up and knocked his pipe out on the bars of the grate. "Well, I wish you luck, Mr Clark, in your search. Good morning."

The stranger refused to take the hint. "There is also a girl," he said. "Information about her would be also rewarded."

Templeton ostentatiously threw the door open and held out his hand. "I'm sorry we can't help you," he said. "Good-bye."

This time the man had no option but to retire.

"What do you make of that?" said Templeton, coming back from showing their visitor to the street.

"I don't know," said Pollock, "but I don't like the look of him. An unpleasant sort of fellow."

Templeton strolled over to the window and stood looking out some minutes, then he turned to his allies and began abruptly, "I don't know how it strikes you fellows, but we are not doing much good at this game. We are no nearer getting Snell and Armstrong back or finding out what has happened to them. I suggest that we chuck it."

Gardiner's face fell and he replied gloomily, "Perhaps you're right. We've got so worked up with this detective business that we have been rather inclined to forget those poor lads. I wonder what has happened to them."

"After all," said Templeton, "we only went into this thing at the beginning for fun. We kept on with it solely to get those two out of whatever dungeon they're in. That being so, I think we ought to advertise and say that after they are returned we will chuck the whole business."

The others reluctantly agreed, and an advertisement appeared in *The Times*, *Daily Telegraph*, and *Morning Post* on the following day:

"To Susan Blake. — If S. and A. are sent back undamaged, we promise to take no further action. — G. T."

The advertisement had an immediate result in a telephone call from Susan Blake herself, asking Templeton to meet her at Lyons' Restaurant in Coventry Street in half-an-hour's time. "There's no good bringing police," she added, "because you won't do any good by getting me arrested."

It was arranged that Templeton should go to the rendezvous, that Gardiner should sit at another table to be at hand if necessary, and that Pollock should be on patrol outside, driving his car backwards and forwards between Leicester Square Tube Station and Piccadilly Circus.

"Don't eat or drink anything," were Pollock's final words to Templeton. "She's the sort of girl one sees at the pictures who slips a little something into your coffee and you wake up at Valparaiso."

The girl arrived punctually. Templeton's first impression was that she had too much lipsalve on her lips. Then he realized that it was the effect of the contrast with her white face which seemed, if possible, even more devoid of colour than usual. She was dressed with perfect taste and she moved across the room with quiet self-possession. Templeton swept a lightning glance over her, from the slight frown that hooded her blue eyes to the silk stockings that displayed a pair of slender ankles. She sat down at the table beside him, crossed her legs and began at once. Without the vestige of a smile or a word of greeting she said, "Well, George. What about this advertisement? Is it honest stuff or a game?"

Templeton replied swiftly, "Honest stuff." She looked very hard at him for an appreciable fraction of a minute. The young man returned the look with as much composure as he could, thinking all the time how uncommonly silly he would feel if he lowered his eyes before the steely gaze of the blue pair opposite. At last she made a slight grimace with her lips and said, "Well, I won't learn anything by staring at you, except that you are good-looking; and I knew that before."

Templeton bowed at the unexpected compliment.

"Were you at a public school?" was the next thing she said.

"I was, Susan, I was. Trained in the British spirit of playing the game, all for the team and nothing for self, never tell a lie, thank God for the Empire, long live the Navy, and three rousing cheers for Joe Chamberlain." Templeton rattled this off at a great rate, more to cover his bewilderment than anything else. To his annoyance the girl, quietly and almost sympathetically, replied: "Talking rot like that gives one time to think, doesn't it?" He flushed a little.

"The trouble about you typical public-school men," she went on, "and I should say you are either Winchester or Eton. . . ."

"Eton."

"The trouble is that idea of playing the game. Because, of course, you decide for yourselves what the game is. In one case it might be playing the game not to tell me a lie. In another it might be playing it to lie on behalf of your friends."

There was a pause during which the girl asked for, and Templeton ordered, a cup of coffee. When the waitress had withdrawn, she put her elbows on the table and leant forward, supporting her chin on the backs of her extremely pretty hands. "Look here, George," she said. "We can't return your friends." Templeton's brow darkened into a deep frown and she hastily added, "No, no, I don't mean that. We haven't done anything so silly as that. They're quite safe. They're on a sailing ship doing a six months' cruise to New Zealand or some such spot. Very healthy and enjoyable. The big one will miss his football but it can't be helped."

"Say all that again," said Templeton incredulously.

"Dear me, how slow you are," she sighed. "When we found that they weren't real spies we gave them a dose of chloroform and put them on board the good ship 'Tromso,' Norwegian, Captain Johansen, bound for the South Seas, cargo of something or other, no wireless on board. Now do you understand or shall I say it in words of one syllable? They're supposed to be patients in need of a long rest, mental cases. It's a pure chance that you aren't a mental case too."

"It's a good story, but how am I to know if it's true?"

"Look up the shipping records. You'll find all about her, date of sailing, number of sails, and so on.

"Come, come, Susan," said Templeton rather impatiently. "You must do better than that. It isn't worthy of your talents. Anyone can look up shipping records. But that doesn't prove that those two chaps are on board the 'Tromso.'"

"Well, they are," said the girl. "You'll have to take my word for it. We'll take your word that you're going to stop spying on us. Is it a bargain?"

"Yes, if I get those two fellows back."

"I tell you they're on the 'Tromso.'"

"Very well. It looks like a deadlock."

"You mean you'll go on spying?" Her voice was slightly metallic.

"It isn't spying. I want my friends back and I'm going to make it as uncomfortable as I can for you all till I get them."

"Well, that's plain speaking. I'll speak plainly too, Mr George Templeton. If you interfere any more in things that don't concern you, you'll get into pretty serious trouble."

As soon as he saw that the girl had lost for a moment her extraordinary self-possession, Templeton instantly recovered his good humour. "Now, now, Susie," he said as one speaks to a child. "Drink up your coffee like a good little girl and say 'Thank you' to your kind Uncle George."

The blue eyes almost shot sparks of fury for the briefest part of a second. Then the girl also recovered herself and said, "Sugar, please, two lumps."

"Well done," said Templeton admiringly. "You're a remarkable person."

She ignored the compliment and went on, "Will you agree to a truce until the 'Tromso' comes to port?"

Templeton laughed. "That would give you about five months' start apparently. We're not so silly as all that. Why are you so afraid of me?"

She eyed him steadily. "You know that surely?"

"No."

"It's my turn to say 'Come, come, George.'"

"No, seriously," he protested. "What have I done that makes me so dangerous?"

"It isn't what you've done, it's what you've seen. You're the only person in England so far as we know who could identify my father."

Templeton stared for a moment and then said, "Oh, that's the lie of the land, is it? Well, why don't you kidnap me too?"

"We will as soon as we've an hour to spare. At present we're busy."

"By the way," he asked, "I suppose it was you who got old Chisholm away?"

She laughed happily. "Such a dear, chivalrous fellow."

At that moment Gardiner reeled up to the table, apparently in the last stages of intoxication. He greeted Templeton as an old friend and implored him, almost with tears in his eyes, to come and have a drink with him. "You were in my regiment. I remember you. Come and have a nip with me; a little nip of whisky," he begged. "Just one for old times' sake; just a small one, not two fingers." He winked swiftly and expertly.

"Go away," said Templeton. "I don't know you and I don't want to. And you're horribly drunk."

Gardiner drifted away, dolefully lamenting the harshness of the world where people would not drink with him. Templeton glanced swiftly round the restaurant and saw Mr Clark sitting at a neighbouring table, sipping a glass of milk. The right-hand pocket of his coat sagged as if heavily weighted. "There's a gun in that pocket," said Templeton to himself. "He must have followed us here. Young Gardiner is a clever chap." "What are you afraid of?" he suddenly said to the girl.

"How do you know I'm afraid?" she returned.

"You're not quite your gay, confident little self," he replied in a bantering tone.

She leant forward across the table. "I'm afraid of all kinds of people," she said. "Up to a few weeks ago everything was all right, and since then everything has gone wrong. People seem to be against us. Well, you won't have a truce?"

He shook his head.

"You're a fool," she went on a little more cheerfully, "but your two friends are perfectly safe and sound. I promise you that."

She got up. "I must be going. Please don't trouble to follow me. It wouldn't do you the slightest good anyway."

She left the restaurant while Templeton paid the bill. He saw the man with the missing fingers get up and follow her, while Gardiner followed him. At the door the girl got into a taxi. Just as it moved off, the man called Clark opened the door and jumped in beside her.

The next moment Pollock brought his car alongside the kerb. They tumbled in and took up the chase.

The taxi proceeded slowly in a westerly direction. It was obviously in no great hurry. The pursuers kept close behind, expecting at any moment an explosion of some sort from the cab. But to their intense and increasing surprise, mile after mile went past and there was no sign or sound of any commotion or disturbance.

"They can't be friends," muttered Templeton. "I swear they're not, and yet they must be or there would have been a frightful row by this time. But if they are, it upsets all our theories." He tried to think out a new theory of the whole affair on the assumption that the girl and the stranger were allies. But nothing seemed to fit.

"It can't be possible," he said at last. "And if it isn't possible, why isn't there a row in that cab?"

Gardiner, who was sitting in the dickey, leant forward and observed, "There's another sportsman following us. He's been on our tail ever since Piccadilly."

The third car in the procession was small but of a high horse-power. The driver and the man who sat beside him both wore big goggles and heavy overcoats and were unrecognizable.

They jogged along the Great West Road at about fifteen miles an hour and passed through Egham and Staines on the road to Ascot.

"There's something fishy about this taxi," said Pollock. "Why does it take such a long drive at such an extraordinarily slow pace? It must be to give somebody time to do something. I wonder what."

He had not long to wait. On a lonely stretch of road in the neighbourhood of Sunningdale, a big lorry, which had for a mile or two made a fourth in the cavalcade, passed the small powerful car and in doing so swung in upon it and struck it a heavy blow on the off front wheel. The impact was such that the light car was sent spinning into the ditch. A loud shout from behind attracted Gardiner's attention and he quickly grasped the situation.

The lorry had not stopped, but was accelerating and bearing down upon them. He shouted a warning to Pollock who had no option but to accelerate in turn in order to avoid being rammed. He shot past the taxi, the lorry thundering behind. The chase lasted for about half a mile and then the lorry suddenly turned up a side road. As soon as the pursuer had vanished, Pollock turned, but it was too late. The taxi had entirely disappeared.

They tried each side-road in turn for several miles on the chance of picking up the trail again, but to no purpose. All that was left was the light car, which was lying in the ditch, and the two goggled strangers standing beside it.

They returned to Clarges Street extremely crestfallen. "We're the rottenest set of sleuthhounds that ever lived," said Pollock. "Every time we tumble into the simplest sort of dodge for getting rid of us. Let's go round to Scotland Yard."

They recounted the story to Inspector Roberts, who set in motion inquiries in the neighbourhood of Sunningdale. "I haven't much hope of anything coming of it," he said. "People as clever as that wouldn't take you to Sunningdale if they lived there, but somebody may have seen the taxi or the lorry. It's an extraordinary thing that you saw no sign of trouble in the taxi when you passed it. The man with the missing fingers should be easy enough to trace, and then there are the numbers of the taxi, the car and the lorry, though again I don't hold out much hope from those. I congratulate you on getting the number of the lorry," he turned to Gardiner. "It's easy enough to lose your head in a case like that and forget all about the number."

Gardiner coughed modestly and murmured, "The others lost their heads. They always do." It was not for another week that they heard again from the inspector. He was looking gloomy when they went round to Scotland Yard to see him. "Unless something happens within a few days," he said, "we are going to drop this case. Either your two friends are dead or else they are on the 'Tromso.' The girl's story is perfectly correct about there being such a ship and about it having sailed, but as it doesn't carry wireless and doesn't seem to touch at any port after passing the Cape, we can't verify the rest of the story until it reaches New Zealand. If they are not on the ship . . ." he shrugged his shoulders. "Every single line of inquiry has been a failure. The numbers on the taxi and the lorry were both faked. Alexandrovski has been watched but has done nothing in any way suspicious. Your friend without the fingers has vanished completely. By the way, we have a very good idea that he is a pretty high official in the Russian Secret Police. He corresponds with the description of one of the leaders in the 1917 revolution. The motor with the two men in goggles belongs to the Russian Embassy, and I imagine that they were Mr Clark's escort. The officials at the Embassy refuse to give us any information about any of the men. They simply say that the men in goggles were out on official business when they met with their accident.

"There has been a general search for a trace of the bombs which the man Morton took delivery of at Euston, and I have also had inquiries made as to where the metal for the bombs came from. There has not been any result." He spread out his hands. "Everything ends in a dead wall, and, as I say, unless something crops up in a very short time, we shall assume that your two friends are on the 'Tromso' until we hear to the contrary. That is the situation."

"All the same," he added, "I shall be very reluctant to drop it. There is obviously so much more in it than meets the eye. Our special branch reports quite remarkable activity in this country and in others. I am told that there is a general feeling of unrest among Balkan refugees; for example, remnants of the 'White Army' which have been stagnating in the Balkans for years have suddenly become full of enthusiasm and are drilling away for all they're worth.

"Then the Spaniards are not too happy about the position in Morocco. The Riffs seem to be getting their tails up again." He threw across a copy of *The Times* to Templeton and said, "You'll have seen that the Syrian revolt seems to be on the point of breaking out again for no apparent reason. Everybody is waiting for something to happen, and I am quite certain that the key to the whole thing was in that farm in Scotland and now is somewhere in England. Well, well, we must just hope for the best."

CHAPTER XII

The Warehouse in the East End

That very afternoon Inspector Roberts' waning interest in the case revived. A small sneak-thief was arrested in the East End of London for loitering with intent to commit a felony, and in his possession was found a Bank of Scotland five-pound note. Such notes are extremely rare in England, and the man was closely questioned as to its origin. He stuck obstinately to the story that he had earned it, but he refused to say how or where.

An incident of so trifling a nature would naturally not have been reported beyond the area of the local police station and the local police court. But the tracing of the note quickly revealed the fact that it had been paid over the counter of the North of Scotland Bank to the proprietor of the Links Hotel. The proprietor replied to a telegram that he had cashed a cheque for Snell some three weeks before, and this note had formed part of the money.

The affair immediately assumed a greater importance. Scotland Yard was notified and Inspector Roberts went to interview the thief. On hearing that a charge of being concerned in abduction would be made against him unless he could clear himself, the man eagerly told the full story. It had been given to him, he said, by a man called Welsh — Jim Welsh — for carrying a tin box from the lodging-house off the Commercial Road East to another house in the neighbourhood of Limehouse High Street.

He offered to guide the inspector to the house, and within half an hour he had led the way to a small, dilapidated warehouse. The warehouse stood in the angle formed by the junction of two streets. There was no entry into it from either street and each wall presented a wide expanse of brick, unbroken save for a single window high above the level of the ground. The windows had once been boarded over with loose boards, carelessly nailed into position, but time and weather and neglect had combined to rot away the greater part of these improvised shutters. At one side the warehouse abutted on to a row of poor houses and similar buildings. On the other the brick wall was continued at a height of about twelve feet for a matter of ten or fifteen yards, ending in another warehouse. In the middle of this wall was a large double gate, once painted green but now weather-worn into a dingy grey. The words "Tomlinson & Stagg, Exporters," could be deciphered across it.

A locksmith was soon obtained to open the gates. Inside was a small yard, the gravel surface of which was heavily rutted with the recent marks of motor wheels, and the door of the warehouse itself. Inspector Roberts knocked loudly and repeatedly; finally he asked the locksmith to open the door for him. As soon as the work was complete, the inspector made a rapid tour of the building. It consisted of two floors connected with a ladder and trap-door. The ground floor was half-filled with square wooden boxes. The inspector mounted the ladder cautiously and opened the trap-door. The upper floor was also packed from ground to roof with boxes.

He descended, and, borrowing a chisel from the locksmith, carefully prized up the lid of one of the boxes. It was full of small metal cylinders. "Mr Templeton's bomb," said the inspector to himself. "That must be the sort of thing he saw on the road. Well, thank goodness for that. We may get a move on at last. I must get Templeton down to identify them."

He returned to the local police station and telephoned for Templeton and for police assistance. The latter arrived first and Roberts posted a guard of one plain-clothes man further down the street at a point where he could command a view of the big gates. Two others with a powerful motor bicycle and side-car were placed out of sight of the warehouse in such a position that they could see the watcher in the street.

Templeton arrived shortly after and promptly identified the cylinders. "Well, that's that," said Roberts. "It's a step forward at last."

"Of course, they're only containers," said Templeton. "They must go somewhere else to be filled with explosive or whatever it is they put in them, and detonators."

"The next thing is to find out where that operation is done," said Roberts. "I have no doubt that our friend Mr Morton will be along soon with one of his lorries. The 'Jim Welsh' who gave the five-pound note appears to be Morton himself. At any rate, the man who got it from him describes Welsh as a very fat, pasty-faced creature, so it sounds like him."

It was arranged that Templeton, Gardiner and Pollock should take it in turn to accompany the plain-clothes policeman in order to point out

Morton if and when he should arrive. Roberts strongly impressed upon his subordinates that in no circumstances were they to attempt to make an arrest; they were simply to follow Morton wherever he should go. The arrest of Morton would destroy the only clue they had.

It happened that Gardiner was on duty on the following afternoon when a lorry arrived at the warehouse. A man sitting beside the driver unlocked the outer gates and the lorry passed inside. Gardiner left his official colleague at his post and drifted down the street under the wall of the warehouse yard. There was a slight curve in the wall so that by hugging it closely Gardiner was out of sight of the policeman a yard or two before he reached the corner where the two streets met.

He looked up at the wall and estimated his chances of climbing it. It was perfectly smooth. There were no crevices which might serve as a foothold and the task was impossible singlehanded. A couple of labourers were passing on the other side and Gardiner hailed them. "Would five bob be any use to you?" He pulled out a couple of half-crowns and clinked them. The men came across with alacrity. "I want to get on to that wall," he said. "Will you give me a back?"

Next moment he was sitting astride the wall, tossing down the half-crowns to the men below. The yard was empty. The lorry had been backed against the door of the warehouse, which was open.

Gardiner wriggled as rapidly as he could along the wall to the point where it amalgamated with the wall of the warehouse. The badly shuttered window had caught his eye. There was no glass behind the boards and Gardiner grasped the window-sill and hauled himself up by his arms. He squeezed through the gap in the boarding and vanished into the warehouse in the nick of time. For the men came out of the door of the warehouse the moment after, carrying a couple of boxes which they loaded into the lorry.

As soon as Gardiner was inside he surveyed his position. He looked back at his line of retreat and the first thing he saw was a Chinaman, standing in the road and staring with every appearance of interest at the amateur acrobat. As soon as he saw that he was in turn observed, he slipped away rapidly round the corner.

The plain-clothes man was also visible at his post and Gardiner thought he could detect the sound of a motor bicycle engine running slowly and smoothly behind him.

The window through which he had entered looked on to the street and not on to the yard and, therefore, he could not see the proceedings of the crew of the lorry. He took off his shoes and with infinite precautions crept across the sea of boxes with which the upper story of the warehouse was packed, until he came to the trap-door. He very cautiously raised the trap about an inch and pushed a small wedge of wood into the opening to keep it up.

Through the hole thus made he could see a part of the floor below, and across the space at intervals one or other of the men at work passed. Two of them were loading the lorry with the boxes, while a third was checking the numbers in a familiar, wheezy voice. "That's my friend of the gas meter," said Gardiner to himself. "I can recognize his dulcet tones."

The work went on incessantly without a pause, but apart from an occasional oath and the monotonous checking of the boxes, not a word was exchanged. "I hope there are enough boxes on the ground floor to fill the lorry," reflected Gardiner. "Awkward if they had to come up here to get some more." But this problem was solved by a gruff voice saying, "That's the lot, guv'nor," and the wheezy voice replied, "Right, take them along and come back as soon as you can. We've got to get the place clear today."

"What's the hurry?" said a third voice.

"Hurry!" said Morton. "I'll tell you what the hurry is. The game's pretty nearly up; that's my opinion, and if we get this lot off we'll be retiring from business."

"Who said so?" growled the first voice.

"Nobody said so," returned Morton, "but I've got eyes in my head and I can use them as well as anyone else. If I see two and two I put them together and it makes four. See?"

"No, I don't," was the answer in rather sulky tones. "It's a paying job and I don't want to see it come to an end. No one's spotted the game, have they?"

"Don't stand about asking questions. Get on with the job. If we have been spotted, then we're for it. You may lay on that. The people after us are a dirty crowd. Come on now. Get a move on." There was the sound of the lorry being cranked up, of the gates being opened and the rattle of the engine growing fainter and fainter. Gardiner listened intently. With a sigh of relief he heard the unmistakable noise of a powerful motor bicycle coming nearer, passing the outer gates and in turn receding.

"The sleuths on the trail," he said to himself. "In the meantime the blood's running to my head, stooping like this."

On the ground floor Morton went slowly from one pile of boxes to another, counting in an undertone as he went. Once he passed in full view of the invisible watcher above and Gardiner saw that he had a small black notebook in his hand, in which he was making entries. On another occasion he had a large sheet of flimsy paper with which he was apparently checking a consignment which had come by rail. The words "Euston . . . O.K. . . . a hundred and forty-four. . . . Series A to DD . . ." were audible.

He panted and grumbled a good deal from the exertion of moving boxes or climbing over them and he kept up a running flow of soliloquy in a low tone. It was this habit of talking aloud which saved Gardiner a good deal of unpleasantness. For after about twenty minutes, Morton said in a louder and brisker voice, "Well, that's that. All O.K. Now for the other lot."

Gardiner instantly guessed that "the other lot" must mean the boxes in the upper storey of the warehouse, in which case a hasty retreat was necessary. He carefully pulled out the wedge and lowered the trap-door silently into place, and crept back towards the window by which he had entered. Heavy steps began to climb the ladder, which creaked and cracked under the strain; they paused half-way up and then continued. By the time the trap-door was thrown back, Gardiner had reached the window and had hurriedly built a little rampart of boxes between himself and the top of the ladder, leaving a faint chink through which he could watch Morton's proceedings. He glanced back through the window and saw that the Chinaman had returned and was standing below, gazing up at the window.

The trap-door slowly opened and the familiar, heavy features of the fat man from 37 George Street emerged. He hauled himself up laboriously and waited to recover his breath for a moment. Then he began again the counting and checking of the boxes, starting at the side furthest away from the window. After a minute a telephone bell rang below, and with much cursing and groaning he descended the ladder.

Gardiner crept nimbly from his hiding place and returned to listen at the trap-door, which had been left open. At first he heard nothing and then Morton's voice said, "That's bad," and again, "You had better clear out and rejoin when the coast is clear," and a moment later, "You'll just have to abandon it. I'm off now." He hung up the receiver and started towards the door of the warehouse. At that moment a car pulled up outside the gates of the yard and there was the sound of fumbling with the lock.

Morton had halted at the sound, in full view of the trap-door. He was listening with rigid intensity. Then he shuffled with remarkable speed across the warehouse and pulled a revolver out of the drawer of an office table. Gardiner could see his fat fingers trembling as he stuffed cartridges into the chambers of the revolver and put a handful in his pocket. There came the grating sound of the front gate being opened and a swift patter of feet in the yard.

The sunlight coming through the door of the warehouse was suddenly darkened and a harsh voice said, "Drop that pistol!" There was a second's pause and Morton dropped the pistol with a clatter on to the floor. Three men stepped forward, each holding a pistol. Gardiner could only see the tops of their felt hats and their overcoats.

"We want you, Morton," said one of the men. The fat man was shaking and his teeth were almost chattering. "What do you want?" he stammered. "We want you, my friend. Come on, quick."

"I won't come," said Morton with some show of determination.

"Oh yes, you will," said the other.

"Where is your warrant?"

"Warrant!" the man sneered. "Do you suppose that we are the police?"

If Morton had been frightened before, his terror increased a thousand-fold at this remark. His jaw fell and he stuttered, "Who are you? What do you want?"

"We want you to take us to your chief. It's no good saying you won't because you will. We've got plenty of ways of persuading you. You're going to come back now with us to our little house, and we will see if we can't persuade you to give us an introduction to the great man."

One of the other three gave a short laugh which echoed horridly in the warehouse.

"What do you want with him?" said Morton tremulously. "I won't help anyone to do him any harm."

"Never you mind what we want with him. Are you coming quietly now?" The fat man, who had collapsed in a flabby heap on one of the boxes, made an effort to rise. Two of the men stepped forward and propped him up under each arm and half dragged, half carried him to the door, the third man standing by with his pistol ready.

Gardiner was peering down at this extraordinary scene, while a dozen different courses of action raced through his mind. He bore no goodwill to Morton, but at the same time it went against the grain to see a man being kidnapped at the point of the pistol with obviously worse things to follow. He was on the point of taking a chance and throwing one of the boxes down the ladder to make a diversion, and at the same time going for help through the window, when a slight noise behind him made his blood run cold. In his interest in the drama below he had quite forgotten his own hazardous position. He looked over his shoulder and saw that one of the loose boards over the window was shaking. Before he had time to move, two small yellow hands grasped the window-sill, just as his own had done, and a slight sound outside showed that the newcomer was scrambling up the wall. Then above the level of the sill appeared the face of the Chinaman who had been standing in the lane before.

For a moment he stared at Gardiner, who stared back at him, then the Chinese put his foot over the window-sill and raised a finger to his lips.

Gardiner felt vaguely that this gesture was intended to convey that he was a friend, and he sincerely trusted that his instinct was right. In any case there was nothing for him to do. The Chinaman dropped noiselessly to the floor and glided with amazing speed and silence across the boxes towards the trap-door. He arrived just as Morton was being dragged out of sight. Without a moment's hesitation he whipped out a big black automatic pistol and shot the unfortunate fat man through the back of the head.

The noise of the explosion in the confined space of the warehouse was shattering; to Gardiner it came so unexpectedly that he could only gaze stupidly at the body which fell with a thud on the floor. The three men below sprang, with the nimbleness of long experience, out of the line of fire into different corners of the warehouse, while the Chinaman, after one glance to see that his aim had been accurate, slipped from box to box back to the window and almost dived over the sill.

His prompt disappearance roused Gardiner to action. Realizing acutely his position, he hastily followed out of the window, dropping from the sill on to the wall and from the wall into the street. He raced round to the plain-clothes man whom he found still standing at his post, uncertain as to what course he could usefully take single-handed. The Chinaman had vanished.

Just as Gardiner reached the policeman, there came a rush of feet from inside the yard and the three men came tumbling out in headlong flight. They sprang into the car that was waiting for them and drove off at high speed.

Inspector Roberts was on the spot in a short time and listened to the whole story. An allstation call was sent out for the Chinaman and another search was made of the warehouse. The fact that Roberts had missed the telephone in his first search was due to the fact that it was carefully concealed by a pile of boxes. The inspector took up the receiver and waited for the voice of the exchange. In a couple of minutes he put the receiver down and said, "Either the wire is cut or else it's a private telephone." He sent off a uniformed policeman for an electrician to trace the wire.

Then the motor bicycle and side-car returned with one of the two policemen in it. He had a failure to report. The lorry driver had apparently seen that he was being followed. He had stopped outside a public-house and one of the men went in; the policeman had waited fifty yards behind. Then the second man had gone into the public-house and neither of them came out. They had slipped out by a back door and disappeared, leaving their lorry load derelict behind them.

"Another clue gone," said the inspector gloomily. "We'll just have to wait for the Chinaman now."

They had not long to wait. The fugitive had run full tilt into the arms of a policeman on his beat. The policeman had indignantly caught him by the arm and asked him what he meant by butting him like that; the Chinaman had made an effort to escape, whereupon the policeman had marched him off to the nearest station. The pistol was found on him and he made no attempt to deny that he had committed the murder.

"The Bolsheviks are the enemies of China," was all he would say. "Morton was my friend. But those men would have tortured him to give up his secret, so I shot him. What else could I do? I am sorry for Morton. He was my friend. But China is my country."

Not another word would he say and he was duly marched off to the cells.

CHAPTER XIII

The Deadly Discovery

Gardiner returned to Chisholm's flat after his adventures in the East End warehouse to find Templeton in a state of considerable excitement. "Look at that, my boy," he exclaimed, thrusting a cablegram into his hand. Gardiner blinked. "Don't be so impulsive. Pour me out a drink and then tell me your story."

"She was telling the truth," said Templeton. "I am very glad to hear it," replied the Oyster primly. "I am strongly in favour of truthfulness, especially in the feminine sex which is not conspicuously addicted to that virtue. Now tell me who she is and what she has been telling the truth about."

"It's the good ship 'Tromso,'" said Templeton. "It struck a gale and smashed a rudder or a bowsprit or something and had to make the nearest port. Snell and Armstrong are on board, perfectly fit and flourishing. The cable's from Snell."

Gardiner's cherubic face clouded. "That's rather tiresome. Of course I'm glad and all that for their sake, but it will be a pity if it means the end of all our fun. I've had a most capital morning and I should hate the idea of it being the last."

"I don't know about fun," answered Templeton slowly. "I hadn't looked at it in that light. My own idea . . ."

"Always glad to hear that someone else has got an idea," said Pollock, coming in at that moment. "I've no doubt that it's a perfectly rotten one. Tell me what it is and then I shall be able to tell you exactly where you've gone wrong." He spoke lightly but his face was grave and unsmiling. He sat down rather heavily in a chair and pulled a book out of his pocket and threw it on to the table.

Gardiner dropped his mask of carelessness and said almost sharply, "What's the matter, Charlie? What's up?"

"I've made a most devilish discovery, Oyster. At least I think I have." He spoke gloomily. "I think I know what they were making at the Gulls' Cove Farm." Templeton sat up. Gardiner did not move but his blue eyes shone alertly. "If I'm right," went on the barrister, "it's a hellish business. I hit on it by pure chance. I happened to read a tiny paragraph, not more than a couple of lines, in the report of a speech in the *Manchester Guardian*. A man was lecturing on the League of Nations somewhere and giving a list of all the things the League has done. I was glancing at it idly and then — bang! I saw the whole thing."

"What are they making?" asked Templeton. Pollock turned to him. "Anthrax germs," he said simply. There was a complete silence, broken at last by Gardiner's low whistle. "Phew!" he murmured. "That's dirty work."

"How do you know?" said Templeton with such energy that the other two looked at him curiously for a moment.

"This lecture," said Pollock, "Stated that the League had stopped the spread of anthrax by stopping the circulation of infected wool and shaving brushes. That's all. Shaving brushes. The rest was easy. What's the weapon that is so small that it can be stored in those barns, that is so light that it will go in that light bomb you found, Templeton? A germ. What germ goes in shaving brushes? The anthrax germ." He leant back heavily.

"But why bombs as well as brushes?" demanded Templeton.

Pollock shrugged his shoulders. "I don't know. Perhaps one is for dropping from aeroplanes and the other is for private assassination."

There was another silence and then Templeton said," Well, I won't believe it till I see it. Look at this cable, Pollock."

The barrister's gloomy face lightened a little as he read it, but the clouds quickly descended again. He got up and walked across to the window and looked down at the street below. Gardiner sat on the edge of the table and stared at the carpet. Templeton scowled at the fireplace.

At last Pollock turned and said, "I don't know about you chaps, but my way is clear. I'm going to do my best to stop the business."

"I'm with you, Charles," said Gardiner, and both of them looked at Templeton. The latter stared at the fireplace and then got up and said almost defiantly, "You'll think me a damned fool, but I can't help wondering what will happen to that girl. They've already got a pretty villainous gang of cut-throats after them and it's a poor look-out for a girl like that. I take it that you propose we should join in the hunt."

"It's not a question of hunting anyone," said Pollock. "It's a question of preventing a rather foul crime. If I've guessed right, that's to say."

"Yes, I see all that," said Templeton, knitting his brows. "Look here, if I join you in trying to stop these germ-growers or germ-producers or whatever you call them, will you join me in seeing that the girl comes to no harm?"

"Most emphatically I will," said Pollock, and Gardiner murmured an assent.

"It implies calling off the police," said Templeton. "You realize that. I'm not going to go into the witness-box against her."

"That's all right," said Pollock. "The only charge against them is abduction, and this cable puts that straight. Your friend Snell is a fairly sensible chap, I take it. Send him an urgent cable asking him to wire to Scotland Yard saying that he doesn't want to prosecute. After all, they've had a nice voyage and we'll club together to pay their return fares. The next thing is to locate Griffin, and we ought to be able to do that fairly easily through Morton."

Gardiner coughed.

"By the way," said Templeton, "why aren't you on duty at the warehouse, watching Morton?"

"Mr Morton has been gathered rather violently to his fathers," answered Gardiner and he briefly recounted his story.

"That knocks on the head the chance of tracing Griffin that way," observed Pollock.

"I've been vaguely evolving another plan," said Templeton. "How does this strike you? When they were making — whatever they were making — in Scotland, they had a farm built like a fortress, with a barbed wire entanglement round it, and they were known in the neighbourhood as a party of scientists. We have got ample evidence that they are still at work. The man Morton's activity, for instance, and the lorry loads of containers. It therefore seems to me that they must have another establishment somewhere in or near London which they prepared in good time in case of emergencies, and where they are now carrying on their business. But if their business is on such a scale that it would arouse suspicion unless they were known to be scientists, they will have to be known as scientists again. In other words, what we have to look for is another nest of eccentric individuals who are interested in bees or in stars or in chemicals or the differential calculus or something of the sort."

"I see what you mean," said Pollock. "It's not a bad idea. Then all we want are three ordnance survey maps and three motor cars. We each take a district, visit all the pubs in it and make inquiries. They know everything in pubs. Capital places, pubs. Let's start this afternoon and meet next Saturday at six o'clock in the lounge of the Piccadilly Hotel to compare notes."

"And there's another thing," said Gardiner. "How did those Bolshevistic-looking people know about the warehouse so quickly? I think they must have followed me down there. They know all about us and it would have been perfectly simple. I'm getting rather tired of this following business. If we start out looking for another scientific establishment, they will simply hang about behind us in big motor-cars. It makes me dizzy."

"Well, what do you suggest?" asked Templeton.

"During the late conflict with what used to be called the forces of despotism and tyranny, I used to fly about in aeroplanes," said Gardiner diffidently. "I have an aeroplane still down at Hendon. If we send our cars down to any aerodrome, we can then go by taxi to Hendon, get into my machine and buzz off, leaving a disappointed trail of secret agents behind us.

"You mean," said Pollock, "that we are to trust ourselves to your capacity as an aviator?"

"That was the idea," said Gardiner.

There was a pointed silence and finally Pollock said, "Well, if you've got sufficient nerve to suggest that, I should think you would have sufficient nerve to pilot an aeroplane, so I think we had better go with you."

They drove out to Hendon and embarked on Gardiner's machine, leaving, as he had predicted, a couple of baffled and annoyed strangers in a small car at the gates of the aerodrome.

They flew to an aerodrome in Buckinghamshire, whence they set out upon their search. On the following Saturday, punctually at six p.m., they foregathered again in the Piccadilly Hotel to compare notes. It appeared that scientists were commoner than they had supposed, and they had come across tracks of a number of enthusiastic amateur astronomers, chemists, and so on. Almost all of them, however, were easily proved to be highly respectable and old-established citizens.

They went through each other's lists, comparing and checking with the help of a "Who's Who" and lists of Fellows of various Royal Societies. There was one place in particular that attracted their attention. Pollock had come across a house near Guildford which seemed to require investigation. He could learn little about it except that it was a large house situated among woods a considerable distance from a road. Its owner had recently returned from abroad and it was assumed that he was a scientist either by hobby or occupation, owing to the reports of the postman on the extraordinary and peculiar smells which he sometimes encountered on taking up the early morning mail. Another point that was strongly commented upon in the neighbourhood was the absence of local assistance required, either in the garden or in the house.

"That's sufficiently like the place in Scotland," said Pollock, "to justify our having a look at it. I think we might drift down again in your aeroplane, Oyster, and see what we can see."

"I've got a friend near Guildford," said the Oyster, "who lets me land in one of his big meadows, and he would certainly lend me a car." Struck by a sudden idea, he got up and walked across the lounge to where a rather shabbily dressed man was consuming a white liquid out of a small glass. He leant over the table with an ingratiating smile and said, "We shall be going again by aeroplane tomorrow, so you needn't bother to follow us. I do so hate to see time and petrol being wasted," and then he turned away before the man had time to reply.

"What was that?" asked Pollock.

"It's one of the sportsmen who are following us, I think," said Gardiner. "At any rate, I heard the waiter grumbling because he had been asked for vodka. If I made a mistake, it doesn't matter."

They reached Guildford next day, making a successful landing in the meadow of Gardiner's friend. He was a man who appeared to be accustomed to Gardiner's vagaries, and he readily lent them a car without asking any questions.

They drove out to the house which had been located by Pollock and, putting the car in a local garage, began to make a few tentative inquiries. As they had expected, very little was known of the inhabitants of the house. The owner's name was Bradley and he was supposed to be a famous scientist. He apparently had been abroad for some time and had only recently come into residence. Inquiries at two or three neighbouring public-houses produced singularly little result.

The house was called Woodridge, presumably because it was situated in a small but dense wood on some rising ground. No one seemed to have seen any of the new occupants of Woodridge, and it was certain that they bought all their stores in London and employed no local assistance at all.

The friends decided to return to Guildford and to make an investigation after dark. They equipped themselves in the town with electric torches, india-rubber shoes and wire clippers in case Woodridge was defended by the same barbed wire entanglements as the farm in Scotland. They then settled down in one of the best hotels in Guildford with newspapers and pipes, to pass the time until dinner.

It was nearly ten o'clock before they started again. They drove to within a mile of Woodridge and slipped the car into a disused lane overhung by trees and brambles. They switched off its lights and, taking as much cover as possible from hedges, folds of the ground, and clumps of trees, they moved expertly across country towards the house. The wood from which Woodridge took its name was encircled by a low stone wall, and a carriage drive led from a side road into the centre of the dark clump of trees. There was a small lodge at the gate, but its dilapidated and forlorn appearance showed that it had been long unoccupied. The old, unpainted, wooden gate was closed.

Templeton led the way over a low wall, the others following in single file. Then on hands and knees the party crept into the wood. A long bank of rhododendrons skirted the carriage drive and lay between them and the house. So thick and dense were the trees and the branches that within a few paces of crossing the wall, the darkness had become profound. Templeton, looking up, could hardly see a glimpse of the sky through the leaves.

They moved forward, at every step groping for trees and other obstacles. Suddenly there came a muffled exclamation from Templeton, an exclamation which sounded suspiciously like an oath. He halted at the same time and Gardiner, who was immediately behind, cannoned into him.

"What is it?" he whispered, and Templeton whispered back, "Either trip-wire or a burglar alarm. It's in the grass here." He pulled out his flash-lamp and very carefully examined the obstacle, screening the light as much as possible by using his hat as a shade.

"Trip-wire," he murmured at last with relief.

"Barbed wire a few inches above the ground. A lot of use that is." With infinite precautions the party crossed the half-dozen strands which had been woven from tree to tree. Gardiner pointed to a dark mass, like a barrel, which was lying at the foot of a tree. "A coil of wire," he whispered. "They are just beginning to fortify the place."

Templeton nodded and moved on again, this time even more carefully than before. Their eyes were growing more accustomed to the intense darkness and they found it easier to avoid the small branches of the undergrowth. Occasionally a twig or a dead branch cracked under their feet with a noise that sounded to their anxious ears as loud as the noise of a field gun. Each time they halted and listened, expecting at any minute to run into a sentinel. But not a sound nor a movement came from the darkness in front of them.

They had gone about sixty or seventy yards when they came to a clearing. The trees ended and they found themselves on the edge of what had once been a lawn. It had long been neglected and allowed to run to seed. Tall grasses and hemlock plants and weeds grew in thick profusion to a height of more than a foot. At the other side of this miniature jungle was the house. The bank of rhododendrons which had screened the avenue from sight came to an end a few yards from the corner of the house, so that the watchers could see the whole of the front of the house and all that lay to the left of it. On the right the rhododendrons completely blocked the view.

The clearing which contained the lawn and the house was roughly circular in shape; the watchers could make this out from the silhouette of the tree-tops against the stars. The house lay across the circle at approximately its centre, and its ends almost touched the wood.

Templeton's first thought was to approach the house by crawling through the long grass on the lawn. Lying in the grass they would be completely concealed. Then it occurred to him that they would leave a dark track behind them where they pressed down the grass and that such a track would be painfully visible if the moon came out and if the night grew lighter. He backed, therefore, into the shadow of the trees and made what is called in military language a flank movement towards the left. This brought them to the point where the circle of the clearing almost touched the end of the house. A thick cluster of bushes provided a perfect post of observation a few yards from the corner of the house itself and commanding a view of the lawn, the front door and the first few yards of the avenue before it curved and vanished behind the rhododendrons.

They wormed their way into the bushes until, lying at full length, they could peer out through the leaves and examine the lie of the land. The building was in complete darkness except for two lights, one burning in a ground-floor room and the other shining upwards from a basement window. There was such an appearance of quiet and tranquillity about the place that only the recollection of the barbed wire in the wood prevented George Templeton from getting up and heading the retreat. For fully half an hour there was no sound except the murmur of branches, the rustling of leaves and the occasional note of a whistling bat. The house, the wood, the whole atmosphere was completely peaceful. Templeton began to argue to himself that even the wire proved nothing. It might be precautions against poachers. It might even be part of a poacher's outfit for trapping rabbits. He was on the point of suggesting a retreat when Gardiner tapped him on the shoulder and breathed in his ear, "Wait here while I go round the house," and he glided away into the wood. He had hardly gone a few yards when the other two heard a muffled exclamation, and the next moment he had returned. Even in the dim light of the stars they could see that his face was white. "I stumbled over a grave," he whispered. "At least, if it's not a grave . . ." he broke off and pointed to the wall of the house nearest them, where three spades were leaning. Templeton shivered slightly, and then Gardiner slipped away again round the house. He returned in about a quarter of an hour with no news. Everything at the back was dark.

Templeton put his lips close to Pollock's ear and whispered, "I'm going to have a look at that basement window." The other nodded and Templeton began to work his way forward, keeping as much as possible, in the shadow of the house. He stopped suddenly at a noise from inside, and lay motionless on his face. A bolt was shot and a chain rattled. The front door opened and a man came out and stood for a moment in the light of the front hall, which streamed out on to the lawn. Then with a wave of the hand, he set off down the avenue and was soon lost to sight behind the rhododendrons.

Templeton had not dared to look up for fear that the reflection of the light shining on his face would give him away, but as soon as the sound of the footsteps crunching on the gravel had died down he began to wriggle forward again. With infinite pains and at the rate of a few inches at a time he finally reached the iron grille which was embedded in the ground to prevent the casual passer-by from falling down into the basement. Peering through the grille, he could see into a well-lit room below. For some minutes nothing happened and then Templeton had a shock.

He had expected at any moment to see someone whom he already knew by sight pass across his field of vision; instead, an unearthly apparition appeared. At first he thought that it had not got a face at all, and then he realized that the head of the creature was covered with a huge yellow sack with two eye-holes. It was like an enormous gas mask. The illusion of unearthliness was increased by the fact that the figure was clad from head to foot in an overall of a yellowish, shiny material, tightly strapped at the wrists and ankles. It wore yellow and india-rubber gloves.

The weird apparition gazed for a moment at a glass tube held close to its eyes, and then vanished. "Well, that's one of the scientists," said Templeton to himself, "and I suppose that's where they work."

He laboriously crawled back to the other two; without a word he beckoned to them and led the way through the wood, over the wall, and into a neighbouring cornfield. Then he pulled out a cigarette case, and with a sigh of relief the three lit up and each took a pull at a flask. Templeton told them what he had seen and then said, "Who was the man who came out of the house? Could you see? The one who went down the avenue."

"Alexandrovski," answered Pollock, and Templeton whistled. "So we've hit it first time. That's a bit of luck. Let's go and pay a formal call."

"You don't think it would be better to wait till tomorrow?" said Pollock.

"I think the sooner the better," said Templeton. "Things seem to move so quickly in these circles that you never know where anyone will be tomorrow. All the same, I don't quite like that grave. You're sure it was a grave?"

"Oh no," replied Gardiner, "not sure, but it was exactly what graves look like and the earth was freshly turned."

"Well, come on," said Templeton, throwing away his cigarette and rising to his feet. Once again they entered the wood and, moving this time with the rapidity of knowledge and experience, in a short time they had regained their observation post.

Templeton stepped boldly up to the front door and pulled a resounding peal on the bell, following it up with a spirited performance on the knocker. He quickly flattened himself against the wall in case of hasty and violent action by the inmates. The echoes of the bell had hardly died away when all the lights in the house went out. There was a tense moment of silence. The rustle of the leaves seemed even louder than before. Then a window was flung up noisily and there came a sound of voices arguing and interrupting each other. One voice seemed to dominate the others and the listeners could hear someone saying, "No, no, no! By Heaven, who's afraid?"

A side door opened and a figure slipped from the house and dived into the wood. A twig cracked sharply, and there came a hoarse laugh from the neighbourhood of the rhododendron bush. Templeton did not stir; Pollock and Gardiner lay motionless, pistols in hand, then the same voice that had spoken at the window spoke again, this time from the wood. "Come on, have a shot," it cried scornfully. "You're a poor crew. Which set of assassins are you? Moscow or Dublin?"

Templeton took a deep breath and decided to take a risk. "Neither," he said, in a clear and distinct voice. "It's George Templeton."

The reply was another laugh. "It would be. What the devil brings you here?" Griffin stepped out into the avenue, an automatic pistol in his hand. Templeton stepped forward from the wall against which he had been leaning. "I want to have a talk with you, Griffin."

"You carry your life in your hands," said the other.

Another voice interrupted the conversation, speaking from one of the windows of the house. "What is it, Jack?" Templeton recognized the voice instantly, though he had only heard it once before at the farmhouse in Scotland.

"It's our old friend Templeton and his amateur spies," said Griffin. He turned to Templeton: "At least, I suppose the others are within earshot?"

"We are indeed," said Gardiner jauntily, rising to his feet and emerging, with Pollock close on his heels.

"Bring them in," boomed the deep voice from above. "I should like a word with them."

The bolts, chains, and locks of the front door were undone and Griffin, with a sardonic gesture of hospitality, bowed them in.

Inside the front door was a second door made of steel and sliding in a groove. It was standing half open. Griffin, having locked the outer door, pushed past them, saying, "Shall I lead the way?" They entered a large dining-room; the table was still covered with the remains of dinner. At the head of the table stood a remarkable figure. It was an old man, at least six feet six inches in height. Long white hair made him look venerable. A tremendous hawk nose and deep-sunk eyes made him look sinister. His huge frame was so thin and gaunt that his clothes hung loosely, but even his years did not make him stoop. He must have been fully seventy years of age.

Two men were standing behind him, clad in the yellow overalls that Templeton had seen in the basement. The girl who called herself 'Susan Blake' was sitting on the right of the old man, playing with a nut-cracker. She looked up as the procession entered, almost indifferently.

"Mr Templeton again?" she said, as he bowed.

"He can't keep away from you," said Griffin; "the candle and the moth." No one answered him, and there was an awkward moment. Then the old man waved to the chairs beside the table and said in a deep voice, "Sit down and take a glass of wine."

Templeton hesitated, but Gardiner successfully put everyone more at their ease by picking up the decanter, looking at the old man at the end of the table and saying, "He looks as if he might be anything, but I doubt if he is a poisoner." He poured out a glass and drank it off at one gulp.

The old man glared at him for a moment and then laughed appreciatively. "Well done," he said. "I like that," then he turned to Templeton and went on, "Now, sir, it is for you to explain."

"Explain what?"

"Your presence in my grounds at night. It is not the first time that you have honoured me in this way."

Templeton, realizing that it would be far better to tell the truth than to try to invent some story, said, "I'll make it as short as I can. We first spied upon you out of pure curiosity, to see what Griffin was doing with bombs in Scotland. We then pursued you with the utmost hostility because you had kidnapped two friends of mine. When we found that my friends were quite safe, we dropped the hostility and returned to curiosity. Then we came to the conclusion that you yourself were in grave danger, so we decided to come and offer you our assistance."

The old man raised his heavy grey eyebrows. "Highly ingenious," he said. "This is your full explanation?"

"Certainly."

"And who do you suppose I am in danger from?"

"Of course, you know that better than I do," said Templeton, "but I think I am right in believing you to be in danger. For example, there was the man who had two fingers off his left hand. He was looking for you. And there were the men who attacked Morton in the warehouse."

"Quite so," said the old man, "and how do I know that you are not on their side?"

"I should not be sitting here if I were. After finding out where you lived, I should not have rung your front-door bell. I should have gone back to Guildford and telephoned for assistance to come and shoot you up."

"That's true," the other admitted, "but if you suppose me to be in such danger, why do you want to expose yourself to it also?"

It was Gardiner who replied. "One must have some excitement. This is the pleasantest excitement we have ever known, and we don't want to lose it."

"That explanation," said the old man, turning and staring at the unabashed Gardiner, "is so fantastic that I think it is probably true. No one in their senses would invent such a reason and expect it to be believed. Yes, on the whole I'm inclined to believe you." He leant back in his chair and surveyed them. "So you are setting out as three knight errants, to rescue age and beauty in distress," he waved a gaunt, boney hand in the direction of the girl. "Well, let me tell you that you come at an opportune moment. We are exceedingly hard pressed." He suddenly leant forward and scrutinized Templeton keenly. "How did you get on our track here?"

"By inquiring exhaustively over the country for a party of mysterious scientists who do not like publicity."

"Were you followed?"

"No," said Gardiner.

"How do you know?"

"Because we came by aeroplane."

Their host chuckled and said, "That was clever of you, but what one has done another can do." He frowned and stared at the table. "We must make another move, I think. There is nothing to prevent them also searching for a retiring scientist. That was a mistake, but I don't see how it could have been avoided." He turned to the two motionless figures in the overalls behind him and said, "It's all right now; you can get on with your work."

They marched out of the room like automatic figures, and the host went on, "I only want another fortnight, Mr Templeton. Can you help me to have a quiet fortnight?"

"What do you want it for, sir?" asked Templeton.

"You don't know?" said the old man in surprise. "I am astonished to find that there is anyone who doesn't know. Thanks to your criminal spying and prying, Mr Templeton, the whole story may be in the scareheadlines of the gutter press at any moment. Your blundering may change the face of the world, or, worse still, it may prevent the face of the world from being changed."

"It was not my blundering at all," retorted Templeton with some warmth, and Gardiner intervened smoothly to prevent a dispute. "By the way," he said innocently, "am I right in thinking I tumbled over a grave out there? Whose grave is it, if I may ask?"

"The grave of a scoundrel, sir," said the old man sternly. "He died a more peaceful death than he deserved."

"Was the unfortunate gentleman," pursued the inflexible Oyster, "who has so lately departed this life, the man who was short of his normal equipment of fingers on his left hand?"

Templeton sprang up, knocking his glass over as he did so, and stared at the girl. She met his look with perfect calmness and steadiness.

"What did you do?" he said stammeringly. "We saw him get into your taxi in Leicester Square. What happened?"

"I broke a bottle of chloroform across his face," she answered coolly. "He threatened me. He slept all the way down here."

"And then you killed him in cold blood," said Pollock. "That sounds uncommonly like murder."

"No, sir," thundered the old man. "We tried him by court martial. He spoke in his defence. He had every chance. But he was guilty of a thousand hideous crimes. He was the servant of tyranny. We found him guilty. We condemned him to death and we executed him. It was justice."

"I doubt if Scotland Yard would take that view," said the barrister.

"The view of Scotland Yard will not be asked," was the stern reply. "That man was one of the chiefs of the Moscow Secret Police. He had more crimes to his name than I have hairs on my head," and he shook his white locks fiercely.

Pollock took a deep breath and then, looking straight at the formidable old man, said, "Is it anthrax?"

There was a complete silence. Then the old man replied simply, "Yes."

"Yes, I am a purveyor of anthrax germs," he spoke proudly. Gardiner stole a look at Templeton. He was very white but he was so composed that the astute young man guessed that Templeton had really expected and been prepared for the answer, in spite of his incredulity when the idea had been suggested.

The old man threw back his head. "I don't know how you guessed it," he said, "but it is true. Have you ever heard of gun-runners? Of course you have. But guns are growing obsolete. The war of the future will be a war of germs. I am a germ-runner. I am De la Rey, the first of the germ-runners, the only one in the world. Through me and my wares Liberty will be finally achieved."

Templeton shuddered. "What a ghastly idea."

"Not so ghastly as tyranny," was the reply. "That is the worst of all crimes, and there is more of it today in the world than ever before, and it is harder than ever before to overthrow. Why? Because of the power of modern weapons. A tyrant with one machine gun is more powerful than a hundred patriots with rifles. In the modern organization of the world it is impossible for the champions of freedom to overthrow tyranny because they cannot get the weapons. But that state of things will end in a fortnight.

I am providing the weapons. No machine gun in the world, no tank, no aeroplane can stand up against the power of the anthrax germ. In a fortnight from today the last and biggest consignment of germs will have been dispatched, and then the work of uprooting the tyrants will start simultaneously all over the world. That is what the shaving brushes are for.

They will play a part; they will be impregnated with germs and dispatched in the required directions. The rest will be let loose in other ways. It is organized to the last detail. In Russia, Ireland, Morocco, Syria, China, Rumania and many other places there will be the greatest uprising against tyranny that has ever been seen. But I tell you, sir, we are hard pressed by the forces of reaction.

"For months there have been rumours that a new weapon was coming, and for months the secret services have been trying to find out what the weapon is and where it is coming from. Thanks partly to you and partly to ill-fortune, they have got very close to us. The capture of the warehouse was a great blow to me. I had no idea they were as close upon our heels as that."

"It's a hideous form of war," broke out Templeton.

"Hypocrisy!" replied the other. "Flabby-minded hypocrisy. It is poor consolation to a soldier if you tell him that you are going to abolish the use of poison gas and leave him to be torn to pieces by shells and bullets. The only way to abolish the horrors of war is to abolish war itself, and that will only be done when the tyrants are overthrown."

"What happens," put in Pollock, "if you overthrow one tyranny and set up another that is worse than the first."

"We shall overthrow that too. You think I am a murderer because I killed that Russian. I had no scruples. It was an act of justice. They that take the sword shall perish by the sword. Why did I not kill your friend Snell if I am a murderer? For no inducement in the world would I have killed him after I discovered that he was not the tool of tyranny. I am not a murderer. I am the Organizer of Liberty. I am the practical Mazzini. I am the new Rousseau."

There was a wild, fanatical gleam in his eye. His great voice rolled and thundered. His bony fingers clenched and unclenched themselves. Templeton slid a glance out of the corner of his eye at the girl. She was sitting, gazing at the old man, with shining eyes and hands clasped. The great, gaunt hand came down with a thump upon the table so that the glasses and silver rattled. "I am the Organizer of Liberty," he said again, and then he fell back in his chair exhausted.

Griffin, who had been standing up listening with an air of polite boredom to the conversation, dropped into the seat beside Templeton and murmured in his ear, "He's had an extraordinary career. An extraordinary man."

The girl turned at last and said with a quick smile, "Well, Mr Templeton, are you still prepared to help us?"

112

"I am prepared to help you in danger, but I am not prepared to help you to flood the world with germs."

Her smile abruptly vanished. "We only want your help for a fortnight. After that, it doesn't matter." She yawned gracefully and added in a languid voice, "I'm not sure that we even want it for a fortnight."

Templeton flushed and was about to make an angry retort when the host opened his eyes again. "Another fortnight," he said. "That's all I want, and then I'll light such a candle as will make Master Latimer's seem a very poor affair." He thumped his chest. "If they get me, then Griffin will carry on the work. It's a race between time and the assassin's bullet."

"Indeed," said Gardiner politely, realizing that it was hardly an adequate reply, but at the same time not knowing what else to say. The old man glared fiercely at him for a moment, but Gardiner was not in the least abashed.

"A race between time and the assassin's bullet," he repeated. "Most dramatic."

"But I am not afraid of assassins," went on their somewhat alarming host. "I got accustomed to them in America. Did you ever hear of Judge Newton of Dakota? He was before your day. I spent years hunting him down and finally I shot him. All the time I was pursued by hired murderers. They never got me. I got him. You ask me why I shot him?"

"I didn't, but I will if you like," murmured Gardiner, but the other was not listening.

"I shot him because he was an unjust judge. Do you remember the killing of Smirnov, the Governor of the Russian province of Vitolsk? He was an unjust Governor and he was blown to pieces by a bomb. I supplied that bomb. Do you remember Smith-Clayton? He was Commissioner of an Indian Reserve in the Middle West. Oil was found on the Indian lands. He introduced brandy and gin into the Reserve. Within a year he had bought the land from the survivors for a few cases of gin. The survivors mostly died of delirium tremens. Smith-Clayton was on the way to becoming a rich man. But he never became rich. I killed him. Just a few drops of strychnine.

"Do you remember Oman Pasha who carried out the Armenian massacres? I shot him in 1911. Did you ever hear of the mysterious series of murders in the Congo rubber plantation in ninety-six? I flatter myself that I caused a certain amount of alarm and despondency on that coast in those years." His eyes gleamed with a mixture of savagery and humour. "The Putumayo atrocities were another case. The story of the fifteen overseers was a pretty one. They were found, fifteen of the worst men who ever oppressed a native population, at the foot of a cliff. All fifteen together. Eye-witnesses who found them said that they must have died horrible deaths. The eye-witnesses were right. They had.

It is one of my greatest regrets that I never have had the time to visit the slave traders of Abyssinia and the Red Sea. But I could not do everything single-handed. I could not be everywhere. I am getting old. Killing one tyrant here and another there is slow work. I haven't time for it. The only thing to do is to kill them wholesale. That is why I have taken to germ-running. The germs will kill in thousands. They begin in a fortnight's time. Give me another fortnight and my work will be complete."

CHAPTER XIV

Woodridge

Griffin, who had been listening to this harangue with a slightly sardonic smile on his lips, looking from one to another of the listeners to see the impression that was being made on each, suddenly lifted his hand and said in a sharp undertone, "What was that?" There was dead silence; everyone held their breath. "I heard something," he whispered at length. Then came an unmistakable sound. "There it is," said Griffin. "It's coming from the shutters of the next room." He tiptoed to the door and noiselessly switched off the light. The sound stopped and then began again. It was a gentle, scratching sound, as if a cat was clawing a piece of furniture. Suddenly Griffin spoke in a harsh and angry undertone. "Are these friends of yours, George Templeton? Have you been playing a game all this time?"

The girl immediately intervened. "Don't be a fool, Jack. Keep your temper."

"I'll go out and see who it is," volunteered Templeton.

"You'll stay here," said Griffin threateningly, and the girl again said, "Don't be a fool, Jack." The door of the dining-room opened gently and one of the men wearing the yellow overalls tiptoed in. "There's someone outside, Chief," he whispered.

"I know," answered Griffin. "Stay here while I go and look."

There was a loud click and Gardiner involuntarily exclaimed, "What's that?" From somewhere in the darkness came a gentle laugh from the girl. "It's only Jack's gun. You must get accustomed to guns."

Griffin had slipped out and shut the door behind him. There was not a sound in the room except the ticking of a clock which seemed to reverberate like a minute-gun, and the fast and difficult breathing of the old man. It sounded as if he were desperately afraid. Then a sound of scratching broke out on one of the shutters of the dining-room itself.

"We do get excitement," said Gardiner in an audible voice which was greeted by a chorus of savage "Hushes." Then one of the window panes cracked across and then fell with a clatter on to the floor. Then Griffin's voice was heard from above shouting loudly, "Who's there?"

There was no answer and the sounds on the shutter abruptly stopped.

The ten minutes before Griffin's return passed very slowly. He finally came back briskly and switched on the light. "Whoever it was has gone," he said. "I've been round the house. I think they must have been trying to push back the catch of the shutter with a piece of wire. Come on, let's go to bed." He turned to the man in the overalls. "You and I will take it in turns to watch. I'll toss you for the first turn."

The old man broke in feverishly. "No, no, Jack. You must work in the laboratory tonight. If we don't keep at it day and night we shall never get finished in the fortnight. I can't spare you for a moment."

Griffin shrugged his shoulders impatiently. "And if we don't watch tonight the work will never be finished at all, in one day or a thousand days."

"The obvious solution," said Templeton smoothly, "is for us to watch." Griffin turned to him with a sneer. "That's a pretty idea — to turn our own pet spies into watchmen so that you can let your friends in at your own convenience."

Templeton laughed. "You always were a pleasant sort of chap, Griffin."

"Oh, if you want pleasantness," said Griffin impatiently, "you'll have to choose some other time. At the present moment we are all in danger of getting our throats cut; that's the thing to remember. When we get out of this hole I'll be as pleasant as you like."

"Allow me to put your position to you," said Pollock in his blandest and most legal manner. "If we are spies, you are done anyway, whether we watch or not. We wouldn't be such fools as to come in here if we hadn't got the whole of Scotland Yard behind us. If we are not spies, then you have still got a chance of getting away. You had better treat us as if we were not spies."

The girl broke in, "That's pure common-sense. Anyone but you would see it, Jack. If they're willing to watch, let them watch."

Griffin looked at the girl with one of his most irritating smiles and then he shrugged his shoulders and said, "All right, just as you like. And look here, Templeton, whatever you do or whatever you see, for God's sake don't do anything rash. There's been enough rashness and folly in this business for the last few weeks. Our only chance is not to let them know they're on the right track. If you blaze off at them, they'll know at once that they're right."

"In any case," said Gardiner, "it might have been poachers."

"Might!" said Griffin. "They might have been pink peacocks for all we know, but it's extremely unlikely." He went on in a matter-of-fact tone. "The best place to watch from is from the upper storey. It's unoccupied, and you'll get a good view from the windows. I'm not afraid of their getting into the place — it's too well protected, but I am afraid of fire. The trees at that corner are so damned near the house." He laughed and added, "not that it matters much anyway; we'll all have our throats cut inside a week." He began to pull on a suit of overalls and then said, as if speaking to himself, "This is the sort of situation in which I regret the absence of the lately deceased Morton. Not particularly for his valour or for his skill in the noble art of self-defence, but for his acquaintances. He certainly had the most magnificently ruffianly crew of friends and each and all of them would do anything for a couple of quid. Poor old Morton! I wonder if there are germs where he is now. I remember you at Trinity, Templeton," he ran on without stopping. "A damned awful prig, weren't you? This knight-errantry stuff suits you down to the ground unless your character's changed a good deal since then."

Templeton kept his temper. The man's insults were too grotesque to be anything but amusing, and his nerves were obviously on edge. But Griffin had amazingly quick perceptions, and he added, "Damn it, I'm a fool. But I am all jumps these days. The old man's a jumpy sort of bird to have about the house." He paid not the slightest attention to De la Rey as he spoke. The girl turned on him with a cold sort of contempt. "You're a bit of a cad, Jack, aren't you?" She was going to say something more when he broke in, "Oh, cut it out, Mary. Don't let's have any more scrapping. We're all on the edge of hell. Except you," he added with a grin.

"You're on the edge of Paradise. But we aren't so lucky." He said the last sentence with such earnestness that the girl instantly softened. "Run along and work, Jack, and be a good boy." He nodded absently. His thoughts were already elsewhere and he strode to the door.

"Good-night, spies," he said over his shoulder. "Say your prayers if you think they'll do any good." He left the room. The old man who had sat motionless and silent since the first alarm, rose slowly to his feet. "Your arm, Mary," he said, "I am tired." He bowed to the three young men and said, "Good-night, gentlemen. I hope you won't regret joining forces with me. It is a noble task." The girl took his arm and they went out together.

As soon as the door had closed behind him, Pollock walked across to Templeton and put his arm on his shoulder. "I know what you're feeling, old man," he said, "and I'm damned sorry my guess was right. But we'll stick to our part of the bargain through thick and thin. We'll see she doesn't come to harm."

Templeton was touched by the sincerity and warmth of his voice. "It's a rotten business," he said, "and I wish it was over. And I wish in the name of God," he burst out, "that Susan or Mary or whatever her name is wasn't mixed up in it. It isn't the job for a girl, especially a girl like that."

"You see the absolute necessity of stopping this consignment of germs?" asked Pollock, with a touch of anxiety in his voice. He was at once reassured by Templeton's answer. "Oh, of course. Whatever happens that must be stopped."

"We've got almost a fortnight," said Gardiner. "So have the other side," replied Pollock gloomily. "And, by the way, talking about the other side, it's high time we mounted guard, or the fortress will be captured by a coup de main. Let's investigate the observation posts."

"Having first filled our flasks from the decanter," added Gardiner.

It was now past two o'clock in the morning and the three friends decided not to keep watch in turns, but to sit up together. They found on the top floor that there were six rooms, three facing the front and three the back. The two front rooms at each end fortunately had windows facing the sides, so that all the grounds surrounding the house were commanded by one or other of the windows. All the windows had Steel shutters.

Templeton took the back of the house, while the other two looked after the front and sides as best they could between them. They had not long to wait before things began to happen. Gardiner soon reported dark figures in the woods on the side of the house that he was watching. They were moving among the trees at the point where the trees came closest to the house, exactly where they themselves had first taken up their observation post.

The other two came and peered out of Gardiner's window. "They're very busy," whispered Gardiner, as they saw the figures flitting rapidly backwards and forwards through the trees. "But they don't seem to be spying on the house any more. It looks as if they were working at something. What about a sally? We might get some valuable information."

"I've had about enough of those woods for one night," said Templeton. "I feel much happier behind these iron shutters."

"Hear, hear!" murmured Pollock. "When I'm up here with a quarter of an inch of steel between me and the outer world, I feel much safer than when I'm lying on my face under a rhododendron bush alone in a hard and cold world."

"You're a faint-hearted couple," said Gardiner. "Well, you can go," said Templeton, "but if you do, you'll go alone."

"It would be extremely awkward," said Pollock thoughtfully, "if they did set a match to the house and we had to make a bolt for it across the lawn under fire. I seldom shine in situations of that sort."

Templeton leant out as far as he dared. "I see no signs of their piling brushwood or anything of the kind against the house, and we certainly would hear it if they were cutting wood or pulling down branches. They're up to something else, I think. But I can't for the life of me make out what it is."

For more than half an hour they could see signs of activity below, but there was no further attempt made to approach the house. As soon as the dawn began to break, Gardiner insisted on reconnoitring. "You needn't be afraid," he said reassuringly. "After all, you'll have me by your side."

They slipped out of the side door and dived into the woods in the opposite direction to the scene of the night's activity, then, making a wide detour, they came round the house. In the half light of the morning they moved cautiously, keeping under cover as much as possible. They found no traces of the intruders until they reached the shrubbery in which they themselves had hidden on the premises. There they found distinct marks of many feet on the damp turf. Bushes had been trampled down and branches broken.

One of the spades which had been leaning against the wall of the house was stuck into the earth among the bushes. A yard further on was the broken handle of another spade. Gardiner stared for a moment and then whistled softly. "Come on, you fellows," he said, and pushed through the undergrowth. The others followed him and next moment the three were standing on the edge of a newly dug grave. It was empty. "This is the one I stumbled over last night," said Gardiner. "They've dug him up and carted him away. That's what they were so busy at." Although all three had been soldiers in the War and had served in France for years, they were not so hardened that the sight of a grave did not give them an eerie and uncomfortable feeling. The thought of the midnight diggers and the removal of the body of the murdered man gave them a shivery sensation. The sound of a bird rustling among the trees made them Jump nervously. The wood seemed to be full of queer things and creatures. The three men instinctively peered round, looking for enemies or ghosts. Then they simultaneously realized that each had drawn his revolver. They laughed rather sheepishly and Pollock said with unconvincing heartiness, "Come, come; we must pull ourselves together."

"What an extraordinary thing to do," said Templeton at last. "Why did they spend the night doing this instead of attacking the house? They must realize that every moment is valuable and as soon as they found the body they must have known they were on the right track."

"I think it's fairly obvious," said Pollock. "They must have been sent down here to look for the house and not to attack it. Suppose that they were simply scouts. They would have orders to locate the place and then to come back and report. They come down here just the same as we did, not quite sure whether they're on the right track or not. They try to look in through the shutters and can't see anything. They stumble by chance on the grave in the wood and they dig it up to see if they can get any information. They find it's their late chief, so they know they're right. What's the next move? They go back and report, of course, and the main platoon of assassins will be on the way down by now."

"That sounds plausible," said Templeton. "I wonder why they took the body away with them. It gives the show away."

Pollock shrugged his shoulders. "They probably didn't think of that. They thought it would be rather a fine thing to take their countryman away with them."

"They certainly are men of action," said Gardiner. "They find a grave and they promptly dig it up. Let's see where they went to."

It was easy to follow the track through the wood. The soft, wet clay which had been thrown up in the digging operations must have clung to their boots, for they could follow the track, partly by the beaten-down grasses and branches, and partly by the stray lumps of clay. The track struck the public road not far from the main entrance. There were marks on the wall which showed where it had been recently crossed. There was even some clay lying on the top of it. In the road outside was a small pool of oil where a motor-car had stood.

"Well, that's that," said Pollock. "Let's go back and report."

Although it was barely five o'clock when they returned to the house, they found signs of activity. Griffin was in the kitchen making tea. He looked up as they came in. "Hullo, my jolly watchmen," he said. "What of the night? Have some tea? I've just come off the night shift in the laboratory; the old man has taken my place. We're not dead yet and that's something," he added.

The watchmen recounted the events of the night. Griffin looked serious when they came to the story of the grave. "By Jove, that's bad," he said. "What a fool I was to bury him in the garden. The whole gang will be down on us tonight." He looked at his watch. "Five o'clock. The sooner we're out of this place the better." He poured out the tea. "Get some of this down your throats," he said, "while you still have them. Another twenty-four hours and we shall all be dead and damned."

"Speak entirely for yourself," said Gardiner primly. "I don't propose to be either dead or damned within twenty-four hours. We Gardiners are a famous fighting family."

"If you were a famous running family," said Griffin grimly, "it would be more to the point. I must go and tell the Chief about it."

He returned with the old man in a few minutes. The Organizer of Liberty had been roused by the news of danger. His eyes were flashing and he spoke energetically. "Action, gentlemen, action! We must retreat at once. There is not a moment to be lost. Only thirteen days more and then we are safe."

"Retreat?" said Griffin. "Where to?"

"Back to Scotland, of course," said the old man. "It's the only place we have left."

"I don't see much good in that. These fellows know about it just as well as they know about us here."

"Defence!" thundered the old man. "That's the reason. We can't defend this rabbit warren in the middle of England; they will burn it down inside twenty-four hours. But the farm in Scotland — that is a different matter. We could hold out there against a rabble like this."

"That's true enough," said Griffin. "We haven't a dog's chance here. Of course, there's another alternative. We might disband and begin again. . . ." He had not time to finish his sentence; the Chief rose to his full height and thundered at him. "Never! Disband when we are within sight of the end? When thirteen days more will see the whole thing in train? Never! We must go to Scotland at once. It will be two or three days before they find out that we are there, and by that time we can organize our defence." He turned to Gardiner. "You said you had an aeroplane, young man?" He went on without waiting for a reply, much like Napoleon dictating orders for the movement of his army. "We have two motor-cars and two aeroplanes. I shall go in our own aeroplane. You, Jack, will go in the other."

"What about Mary?" said Griffin.

"She will have to come up by car. Nothing must stand in the way of the work. The laboratory staff must come first. We will be able to pack enough stores and laboratory equipment in our aeroplane to keep us going until the motors arrive. These two young men can drive up the cars; my daughter can go with them. Come! Start packing. We will get off at once."

"What about the two mysterious gentlemen who wear such unbecoming clothes?" said Templeton.

Griffin stared at him without understanding, and then he laughed and said, "Oh, you mean the laboratory assistants, Bevan and Grew. Bevan is the pilot of the aeroplane. He was the man who searched for you the first time you came to the farm."

"Grew must pack in with you, Jack, into the second aeroplane," broke in the old man. "We must get the staff to work as soon as we arrive."

The crisis seemed to have infused him with a new energy. He was no longer tottering, but walked as briskly and vigorously as he talked. He was on the point of leaving the room when a thought struck him and he turned to Templeton. For a moment he dropped his domineering, dictatorial tone and became a courtier. "You may think it odd, sir, that we first kidnap your friends, then make use of you as watchmen, and finally in a crisis depart by aeroplane, abandoning you to fight a rear-guard action. I would have scruples about it if I did not know that you are rendering a great service to humanity." He gave an old-fashioned bow and abruptly left the room.

Templeton turned and saw that Griffin was grinning at him. "What's the matter now?" he demanded.

"Your services to humanity," answered Griffin. "Does it give you a glow of righteousness?"

"Very far from it," answered Templeton. "I can't see how I'm serving humanity at all in helping to let loose a lot of infernal germs."

"Never mind," said Griffin. "You'll go down to posterity as a Sub-Organizer of Liberty. I'll bring round the cars. I take it you both can drive?" They nodded and he left the room.

"This is a most infernal mix-up, Pollock," said Templeton.

"You're quite right," said Pollock, "it is."

"We've put ourselves in a most awkward position — either we've got to abandon these people to their fate, and by all appearances their fate will be a particularly unpleasant one, or else we've got to aid and abet in what seems to me to be about the most dastardly thing I've ever heard of."

"The only consolation," said Gardiner, "is that we also have thirteen days before us. So far as one can make out from the old gentleman's conversation, nothing is going to happen until they're ready to loose off the whole lot simultaneously. So we need not make a decision immediately. There's no reason why we should not help them for the next few days. We shall probably get an opportunity of collaring the last consignment and dumping it into the sea."

"Can't we fetch in the police?" said Templeton, and Pollock shook his head.

"I don't think it's a criminal act to tinker with germs."

"No, there's nothing for it," said Templeton, "but to keep in with them for the next few days. We shall have a jolly journey up to Scotland, I think,"

CHAPTER XV

By Hispano-Suiza
to Scotland

For the next hour the whole household was busy packing. Griffin brought round the two cars, two Hispano-Suiza limousines of great power. The main part of the luggage consisted of a number of suit-cases and fourteen packing-cases, each about the size of a case of wine; they were light, but strongly built. Griffin helped to pack them into the back of one of the cars.

Bevan, who had changed from his yellow overalls into ordinary clothes and looked like an ordinary man instead of a troglodyte, departed on a motor-bicycle to tune up his aeroplane which had been stored in the village, while Gardiner retrieved the car in which they had come on the previous night and drove to his friend's house to fetch the second aeroplane. Griffin had pointed out a large field at the back of the house where an excellent landing could be made.

When the aeroplanes arrived, the old man, who had been in a fever of suppressed excitement, insisted on immediate departure. Several small cases and instruments and material for the laboratory were packed into the machines, and then one after another the aeroplanes rose from the ground and set off on their long journey.

Griffin waved a farewell and shouted, "Don't let them shoot into the back of the motors. Even a germ will turn, you know."

Templeton and Pollock were left to do the final clearing up, and at last the two heavily laden cars started. Templeton drove one with the girl beside him, while Pollock was alone in the other. They had decided to go through London and pick up clothes and letters.

They had hardly proceeded more than a mile in the direction of the London road when a motor-bicycle and side-car which had been standing under a hedge fell into line behind them. Templeton, who was driving the second car, saw at once that they were being followed. He accelerated and passed Pollock, and then pulled up in the middle of the road.

"What's the matter?" shouted the barrister, coming to a halt behind him. Templeton jumped out and said briefly, "Same old business. We're being followed again."

Pollock laughed. "Well, we've been taught already how to deal with followers." He looked over his shoulder; the motor-bicycle had come to a halt a hundred yards behind. "All we have to do," he went on, "is to get the bicycle in front of us and then we can just push it into the ditch."

The simple plan worked admirably. They accelerated to a speed of about fifty miles an hour until they came to a sharp corner. As soon as both cars were round the corner they applied the brakes violently and came to a standstill. The motor-bicycle, which had been tearing along in pursuit, was not prepared for the sudden stop and passed them. Next moment the powerful cars had started again. The road was empty and they drove side by side after the motor-bicycle. The driver of the bicycle looked anxiously over his shoulder and realized the significance of the manoeuvre. But it was too late. The cars bore down on him and he took the only possible course, which was to swerve into the ditch. The side-car tipped up, and the last Templeton and Pollock saw of it was a wheel in the air and the figure of a man trying to extricate himself from a patch of brambles and nettles.

They picked up a change of clothes in London, and by noon were moving steadily and smoothly up the Great North Road. They reeled off the miles on the perfect surface with the utmost regularity. Templeton and the girl hardly exchanged a dozen words until they halted for lunch at Stamford.

They were all hungry and ate the first part of their lunch in silence. At last Templeton said, "Well, we seem to have shaken them off."

"We've certainly got rid of them for the present," said Pollock. "There's been nothing behind us since London."

Conversation languished again and then Templeton suddenly said to the girl, "I think the whole business is perfectly horrible."

She stiffened perceptibly and then answered coldly, "What business?"

"These germs," said Templeton. "Don't you think it's horrible?"

"No, I don't," she answered. "I think the end justifies the means."

"How can you possibly tell that?" said Templeton. "How will the means work? You haven't the faintest idea of what will happen. Have you made any arrangements about stopping the disease once you've started it?"

"It will work itself out," said the girl, almost sullenly. "Epidemics always do."

"That's pretty vague," said Pollock, "and mighty poor encouragement for the people who are going to get it."

She turned on him defiantly. "It will be time enough to talk about stopping it when we have got it started. That's the most important thing."

Templeton put his elbows on the table and looked at her steadily. "I simply can't understand," he said, "how anyone like you could take part in such a hateful enterprise."

The girl had quickly recovered her temper and simply said with a sweet smile, "I've no doubt there are lots of things you can't understand."

Templeton shrugged his shoulders. "Well, I'm afraid I don't like it."

"Dear me, what a blow," she replied in a bantering tone.

"It surely isn't too late to chuck it?"

The girl gave a heavy sigh and answered with a sort of tired scorn. "You are such typical public-school men. You all think exactly the same. If a thing isn't cricket, it shouldn't be done. You are always talking about fair play and playing the game and all that sort of rubbish."

"I think germs is a dirty business," said Templeton obstinately.

"You were both soldiers?" she answered. "In the war?"

They nodded. "Well, didn't you have bullets and bombs and gas and all kinds of horrors? Why not have germs? They are no worse than any of the others. As a matter of fact, I think they're much more humane."

Pollock laughed. "You think that's funny," she went on, "That's only because you have got the public school mind, but if you ever thought for two minutes you would see that I am right."

"If I thought for two years," said Pollock, "or twenty years, I wouldn't think differently from what I do now. I think the whole idea emanates from the brains of a set of criminal lunatics."

Her eyes flashed for a second, but she kept her composure. "Thank you," she said, with a little bow, "and may I ask why you have butted in on our affairs if you feel so strongly about it?"

"Simply in order to save you," said Pollock, "from the inevitable consequences of your amazing conduct."

"Nobody asked you to. I don't care two straws whether you save us or not. But if you will help us until the campaign is launched, that's another matter. That would be help worth having."

"Just one question," said Templeton, looking at his watch. "We must be moving on. Do you really believe in this as much as your father does?"

"Yes," said the girl simply.

Templeton frowned. "And what will you do if the thing fails?"

"Nothing. If it fails we shall all be dead."

"It might fail," persisted Templeton, "and you might still be alive."

"No." She smiled gently and tolerantly. "The only way they can stop us is by killing us all."

Templeton seemed about to say something more but stopped and got up. "It's time we took the road again," he said with a yawn. "I'm tired. Driving all day after being up all night is a tiring business."

They continued their journey in silence. As the evening wore on, the traffic on the North Road lessened and they were able to go faster than before. They halted finally for the night at Carlisle. All three were very tired. The girl declined to eat any dinner and retired to bed at once.

Pollock and Templeton hardly exchanged a word until they had lit a couple of cigars and had ordered coffee and brandy. "Well, what about it?" said Templeton at last. "I could do with a sleep, but I think we had better get to work at once."

They went round to the garage and got out the two cars. A few inquiries elicited the fact that there was a river at no great distance. They selected a part of the river which ran through a deserted neighbourhood and drove the cars up to the bank. Then with a screwdriver and a spanner they prized open one of the cases. It was filled with small glass bottles, each carefully packed in a separate compartment lined with cotton wool. Templeton very gingerly extracted one and held it up to the lamp of the car. It contained a muddy liquid.

"Ugh!" said Pollock with a shiver. "Chuck the damned thing in and see if it sinks." Templeton tossed the bottle into the river. It sank at once. The sinking of the bottle was like the breaking of an evil spell. They attacked the packing cases furiously and in a short time the foul cargo was at the bottom of the river. They filled up the boxes with earth to correspond roughly with the weight of the bottles, nailed down the lids again and returned to the hotel.

"There'll be a thundering row when that's discovered," said Templeton as they put away the cars.

"Yes," said Pollock with a grin. "We'll have to be ready to do a pretty quick hundred yards. I only hope the germs won't poison the fishes."

"I don't think so," said Templeton. "Griffin said that the slightest moisture would ruin them."

"All the same," said Pollock, "I fancy old man De la Rey will be a little annoyed with us." They laughed and parted for the night.

Early next morning they started on the last lap of the journey and made fast time as far as Perth where they stopped for petrol and newspapers. One of the first items of news in the *Scotsman* was the murder of Alexandrovski.

His body was found by a farm labourer in a field near Guildford. He had been stabbed in the back. Apparently the assassin had removed all papers from his pockets but the body had been identified by a hotel keeper in the town.

The girl received the news without a single flicker of the eyelid. "I'm sorry," was all she said. "He was a good man and a hard worker."

Templeton looked at her curiously. "It doesn't seem to worry you very much."

"Why should it?" she answered. "Lots of men are going to lose their lives before the work is finished. One more or less makes very little difference, but I say again that I am sorry. He was a patriot."

"What was his job?" asked Pollock.

"There's no harm in telling you now," she replied. "He was the head of the British section of the anti-Bolsheviks. We did all our transactions through him. He came down to Guildford to see about taking delivery of the final consignment."

"What will you do now that he is dead?"

"I don't know," she said simply. "My father makes all the arrangements."

"Another thing I've meant to ask you. What was it down at Winchester?"

"The detonators for the bombs. They were being made there." She smiled for a moment. "What news of Sir Alastair?"

Templeton grinned. "We've had thirty-one Marconigrams from him since he left."

It was a very tired trio that drove up that evening to the barbed wire fence round the Gulls' Cove farm. The journey had been uneventful, with no signs of pursuit or obstruction, but nevertheless all three were very glad that it was over. The constraint in their relations had made conversation difficult. The dumping of the cargo in the river had exercised the most remarkable change in the spirits of the two young men and they had to be very careful to conceal their light-heartedness. A sudden change would have been suspicious and they had the unpleasant feeling that Susan's blue eyes missed very little.

They found that the advance guard of the party had arrived safely, the aeroplanes having behaved beautifully. Work was already in progress in the laboratory, while Gardiner was lounging about, smoking a pipe and admiring the view. The two aeroplanes had been stored in the large garage which had formerly housed one aeroplane and the motor-lorries.

After a cold supper the three friends found themselves for a few minutes alone on the edge of the cliff. Gardiner was rapidly put in possession of the facts of the situation and it was hastily agreed that the remainder of the consignment of germs was to be intercepted at all costs.

There was no sign of any of their hosts that evening and the motorists retired to a welldeserved rest.

Next morning the first task was to unload the motor-cars and deposit the packing cases in one of the barns. This was successfully done without the substitution being detected. Then a council of war was held. It was decided that Pollock and Gardiner should take one of the cars and go to the nearest town to buy provisions and some extra coils of barbed wire in order to strengthen the defences of the farm.

On their return the three friends were to undertake the extra wiring, and were to act as watchmen. De la Rey, Griffin, and his two assistants would thus be free for steady and unceasing work in the improvised laboratory.

"There are only eleven days more, gentlemen," said the old man. "If we can keep them off for eleven days everything will be saved."

"What happens on the eleventh day?" said Gardiner.

"I am expecting a steamer," replied the other, "to come for the final cargo. It is due here on that date. As soon as we have loaded it up our task will be complete." His deep eyes smouldered with excitement and a fierce joy.

The expedition into the town was uneventful and the three friends spent the rest of the day in strengthening the barbed wire entanglement which surrounded the farm. Although some years had passed since the end of the war, they found their skill in the making of entanglements rapidly returned to them, and in the evening they were able to survey proudly quite a formidable obstacle.

One of the suit-cases which had come up from the house near Guildford contained a dozen pistols and several hundred rounds of ammunition, and the armament of the house also included two Service rifles. The old man insisted on keeping one of the rifles himself. "I was once a good shot with a rifle," he said, marching off with it under his arm. The remainder was divided among the garrison. The girl refused a pistol. "I will leave the fighting to my brave protectors," she said with a faint smile.

They divided the watch into shifts — one on duty to watch the land side from one of the upper windows of the farm, the second to watch the sea, and the third to rest. They hardly saw the girl, who was busy all the time doing the cooking and the housework. The scientists worked away in the long barns.

The next day and the day after passed uneventfully. The weather was gloriously fine and hot. It was a curious existence, hanging about and waiting for something to happen.

As each day passed the spirits of the old man rose perceptibly. He kept on rubbing his gaunt hands together and murmuring to himself, "We shall do it yet."

The watchmen did not relax for a moment their vigil and they became thoroughly tired of staring across the fields and the distant moor, and listening to the sound of the seabirds on the cliff. On the fifth day after their arrival a small steamer came slowly towards the shore, and hove to at no great distance from the farm. A stream of flags was run up to the masthead and a small boat put out for the shore. Templeton, who was on the sea watch at that time, called Griffin, who scrutinized the boat and the steamer through field glasses. "That's the boat we're expecting," he said frowning, "but it's five days too soon."

"You're quite sure it's not our opponents," said Templeton.

"Quite sure," said Griffin, staring at the oncoming boat with a perplexed scowl. "I can see our friend the Captain coming ashore." He muttered something inaudible and, turning sharply, went into the house. He returned with the old man, talking to him rapidly in an undertone. The rowing boat grated on the shingle below and a man started to ascend the winding path up to the top of the cliffs. On reaching the top he proved to be a tall man of about forty, with a reckless, devil-may-care expression and a brisk, alert manner. A scar across his cheek and a shifty, roving eye added to the general impression that the Captain might be a useful companion in a brawl but not a very trustworthy one in a financial deal. He strode forward with his hand outstretched; the old man took it rather reluctantly, Templeton thought, and winced at the powerful grip. "You're five days too soon," he boomed at him.

"Give me some whisky," was the somewhat unexpected answer. "I'm as dry as a bone." Griffin went in without a word and returned with a bottle and a glass.

"What does it all mean?" thundered the old man, but the newcomer simply waved his hand and drank half a tumbler of neat whisky. "That's better," he said. "Now what's your trouble?"

"You have come too soon," reiterated Griffin. "That doesn't matter a damn," was the airy reply. "Give me what cargo you've got and I'll be off."

"The cargo isn't ready," said the old man.

"Not ready?" said the Captain. "If it's not ready now it may never be ready. I tell you people are getting jolly suspicious. You say I'm early. No wonder I'm early. I was lying snugly in Reval harbour a few days ago when in came a gunboat that I didn't like the look of. I slipped off in the night and I ran into another gunboat outside. I smelt a rat, I tell you, so I came along as quick as I could."

"What are you frightened of, Captain?"

"I'm frightened of piracy on the high seas," was the cheerful answer. "Those fellows wouldn't think twice about coming aboard and cutting every throat on the ship. You see," he winked an eye, "nobody would be very sorry if my ship and I went up in smoke. I don't think there would be any diplomatic protests." He refilled his glass. "Come on now, Mr What's-your-name, give me what cargo you've got."

"I will not," said the scientist. "The whole essence of the plan is a simultaneous surprise. Not one single movement is to be made, not one single germ is to be let loose before everyone is ready on the appointed day."

"I know all that stuff," said the Captain impatiently. "But what will happen to your scheme if I hang about here for another five days and then get chased away without any of the cargo on board or get pinched and lose the lot. It would be better to get half of it sent over than none at all."

"If I give you half the cargo now," said the old man, "you'll clear out now while it's safe and not come back again for the other half."

"Oh, shut up!" said the Captain in a disgusted tone. "Talk sense."

The old man drew himself up majestically and struck the palm of his left hand with his fist.

"Keep a civil tongue in your head," he boomed.

The sailor drained his glass and said, "Keep calm or you'll get apoplexy. Where's that bottle? There's no good saying you can't trust me, because you've got no other way out of it. You must trust me. Get a chair and sit down and be sensible. Otherwise you'll burst."

"He's talking sense," said Griffin rather sourly. "We'd better give him what we've got and trust him to come back for the rest."

"You can trust me all right," said the Captain. "I'd do anything for money, as you know very well, Jack Thingummybob."

Gardiner, who had been listening to this spirited dialogue, interposed in his gentle voice. "Surely it would solve the problem if you transferred your laboratory to the steamer and finished your germ-growing on board."

"That's not a bad idea," said Griffin. He turned to the sailor. "Our chances of having our throats cut here are about twenty-five to one. What are the chances on your ship?"

"Oh, about fifty to one," he replied flippantly, "and in any case I don't want you. Not unless you alter the terms. But seriously, after all you've got police to protect you here; no one wants to protect me — my reputation is too bad. I think you would be safest if you stay on land. I tell you what I'll do. I'll hang about not so very far away and if you're attacked and I'm not, I can always come in and take you off."

He went to the edge of the path and roared down for his men to come up. Half-a-dozen seamen came up and carried the packing cases down to the boat. De la Rey went indoors, leaving Griffin to superintend. When the last packing case had been shouldered and taken down the narrow path, the Captain turned to Griffin and slapped him heartily on the back. "Now, my lad," he exclaimed, "pleasure after business. Fetch out another bottle of whisky, stick one of these weeds in your face and trot out the damsel." He threw his cigar case at Griffin who was scowling ferociously. "And take that damned thundercloud off your dial," added the Captain. "You ought to be glad to see me. Where's Mary?"

"That's no business of yours," snapped Griffin.

"I didn't say it was business," retorted the Captain easily. "I said it was pleasure, my boy. Mary," he shouted, "there's an old friend to see you."

"You're an infernal swine," muttered Griffin.

"Fetch the whisky," was the reply.

The girl came to the door of the farm. She was wearing a blue and white check apron and in her hand she was holding a saucepan.

"Mary, my angel," said the Captain, "you're looking a perfect . . ." She interrupted coolly but decisively. "Good-morning, Captain Arthur. Did you want anything? I am busy cooking."

"A kiss, that's all." Griffin clenched his fists and took a step forward, but the Captain paid no attention to him.

The girl looked at him with half-closed lids and then she said, "Give him some whisky, Jack," and went back into the farm. Captain Arthur looked after her for a moment. Then he laughed, turned on his heel and went down the path to his boat.

The next day passed without incident and the spirits of the garrison rose prodigiously. Even Griffin was inclined to admit that their chances of surviving the fortnight were looking slightly better than they had been before. He refused to allow that they would all survive, but he conceded that there might be a chance of one or two of them escaping with nothing worse than a bullet in the arm or leg.

The girl maintained an inscrutable silence during these days. She worked in the kitchen and on the rare occasions that she snatched a rest from her duties she sat on a chair and looked over the sea. She refused to respond to conversational openings and contented herself with mono-syllabic replies.

The queer, ill-assorted garrison had almost settled down to a peaceful and routine existence, interfering as little as possible with each other. Templeton realized that although the farm was a small place he had only twice seen the laboratory assistants. They seemed to sleep, eat and work in the barns, and hardly ever emerged. He once asked Griffin to tell him about these extraordinary workers but Griffin only grinned.

On the seventh day Templeton was taking the afternoon watch when he saw a man swinging down the main road and halting to lean over the dyke and look at the farmhouse. He surveyed him through field glasses but could see nothing suspicious. The man remained for a long time motionless, and then he continued walking along the road until he was lost to sight over a slope.

Nearly an hour later he returned along the road, looking attentively over his shoulder at the farm as he walked.

In the evening a postman came down the cart track towards the farm. He was brought up short by the barbed wire fences, and he stood perplexed for a moment. Then he shouted in a loud voice, "Is there anybody there? I've got a registered letter."

Templeton turned his field glasses on him through the loophole which had been arranged in the window curtains. There was not a sound or reply from the farmhouse and the postman shouted again; then he began to walk round the outside of the wire defences. Templeton idly watched him making the circuit. As it was essential that their return to the farm should remain unknown, it was of course out of the question to take in a letter. The postman would have quickly spread the news that the occupants had returned.

He halted at each corner and raised his shout again. Finally he returned round the wire and after a last searching look at the buildings turned away. Templeton suddenly saw with a thrill of astonishment that the man was wearing pointed, patent leather shoes. He scanned him again but could see no other incongruity in his costume, but the shoes were conclusive proof. No postman wears anything but boots. No one whose occupation consists in walking twenty or thirty miles a day over country roads wears thin, flimsy shoes which would be suitable for a dancing floor. Templeton watched him retreating, and now that his suspicions were aroused, could see, or thought he could see, that the man had not the long, methodical stride of an experienced postman. He watched him out of sight and then went downstairs to find Pollock and Gardiner.

CHAPTER XVI

Sea-borne Visitors to the Factory

His two friends were lounging in the sitting-room, ostensibly keeping a bored and languid eye upon the sea, but actually reading back numbers of illustrated papers. Griffin was sitting astride a chair, eating bread and cheese, and drumming on the back of the chair with a knife. Templeton described the postman and Gardiner whistled. "That's one for you," he said. "I couldn't have done it better myself." He patted Templeton on the shoulder in a condescending manner. "Let's hope something will happen now; I'm getting a bit tired of this knight errantry business with nothing happening. I've come all the way up to Scotland to rescue a damsel in distress and there doesn't seem to be any distress. Altogether most provoking."

Pollock removed his pipe and said thoughtfully, "I wonder if your postman friend spotted that we were in residence."

"I don't think so," said Templeton. "He looked rather baffled."

"Well, then, in that case," said the barrister, "I imagine that there will be another reconnaissance in force tonight and I should think that it will come from the sea. They probably won't like the look of barbed wire."

Gardiner turned with a plaintive air to Griffin. "Why haven't you got a gang, Mr Griffin?" he said. "All the best crooks have got gangs, at least so I understand. Here you are, letting us in for a most dangerous situation, and you haven't even got a gang ready to help."

Griffin went on munching. "I like that," he said, between bites. "Where is our gang, indeed? We had a perfectly good gang before you chaps came along. But it's all split up now. One of them is in Inverness Gaol for carrying fire-arms. Morton has been gathered to his fathers and all his pals have gone to ground. One of them ran into your friend and got chucked over the cliff. Where is our gang? You may well ask." He took a deep pull of beer from a tankard beside him and then added, "Not that it would matter anyway. We shan't be long on this planet."

"You're a cheery sort of chap," said Gardiner. "By the way, what happened to the gentleman who fell over the cliff?"

Griffin jerked his head towards the sea. "Stone round his neck and another round his heels. Full naval honours. Jolly nearly did the same for your two friends as well." He got up and began to pull on his rubber gloves again, preparatory to going back to work.

"I say," said Templeton suddenly, "why didn't we get some help from that steamer? The captain seemed a decent sort of chap."

Griffin turned with a scowl. "He's an untrustworthy swine," he said. "He'd do anything for money, any mortal thing under the sun. Take my advice and don't have anything to do with that fellow. Besides, he's an old Harrovian."

"He seemed so pleasant," said Gardiner.

"Yes, because he hasn't been paid," retorted Griffin. "He doesn't get his money till the end of the voyage." He went out and Gardiner murmured, "There seems to be no love lost between friend Griffin and the captain."

"It's only because Griffin was at Eton," said Templeton. Gardiner shook his head. "I doubt if that would account for so much venom."

"Well," said Templeton, "it's time we made arrangements for the night. We had better all three be on duty. I suggest that Pollock takes the land side and Gardiner and I the cliff."

They had spent some of the time which had hung so heavy on their hands in digging a semi-circular trench round the top of the cliff overlooking the sandy beach. The only part of the frontage which they had not dug was a space a yard wide for the path which ascended from the beach to the farmhouse door.

As darkness fell Gardiner and Templeton took up their posts in the trench beside the path. It was constructed on the model of a trench in Flanders, complete with parapet, fire-step and occasional loophole. When standing on the fire-step they could command an excellent view of the steep slope down to the beach. The two sentinels laid their pistols on the parapet in front of them, lit their pipes and lay back against the wall of the trench.

"Just like being at the war again," said Gardiner. "It reminds me of Plug Street in '15. Were you ever at Plug Street?" Templeton laughed. "Yes, I was indeed. Jolly spot. Did you know Brielen?"

"You mean in the salient?"

A long exchange of reminiscences followed, ranging from Dixmude to Amiens.

"And here we are at it again," said the Oyster finally.

Templeton nodded. "It's a remarkable change from my first visit to this cove," he said. "We came round that corner there, spying on the farmhouse, and now here I am entrenched up here defending the very people that I came to spy on. And I must say," he added thoughtfully, "the people that we're helping are not particularly enthusiastic about our help."

"Well, they would be in a pretty hole if it wasn't for us," said Gardiner.

There was a footstep on the gravel behind them and Pollock dropped into the trench. "Hullo, hullo," said Gardiner. "Leaving your post is a pretty serious crime. I'm not at all sure we couldn't have you shot for that."

"It's an idea that's just occurred to me," said Pollock. "A very awkward idea."

"What about your post?" persisted Gardiner, but the barrister waved his hand airily.

"Nothing doing on the Western Front. It's much lighter at the back than it is here. Nothing will happen on my side for a good time yet. Look here. This is what I've been thinking."

"We've already intercepted one consignment of germs and dumped it at the bottom of that river. If we intercept the next lot also, these friends of ours will be treated as traitors by their own side. People will think that they have simply taken the money and sent them dummy consignments. Then they'll have both sides against them."

Templeton moved impatiently. "Confound it, Pollock," he said. "That's their look-out. We can't go into every single detail and every possible consequence of their actions, past and present and future. It seems to me that the only thing we've got to do is to make quite certain that these consignments never get sent off. I take it that's what we're here for?"

"But, I say," said Gardiner, "what about the girl?"

"I'm going to do my best for her," said Templeton doggedly, "but she will have to be ready to fend for herself."

"But I thought it was for her lovely eyes that you were — how shall I express it?"

"You needn't bother to express it at all," interrupted Templeton, flushing, "because it's all rot. I never met anyone more capable of looking after herself."

"Well, well, well," said Gardiner, "this is a disillusionment. I had fully expected to be attending at St Margaret's, Westminster, in spats and silk hat, while bride and bridegroom walked out under an archway of germs. What a disappointment!"

"Shut up, Oyster," said Pollock.

"A little less impudence from you, please, Mr Pollock," retorted the young man, "and if that's finished your gossip it's time you were back at your post. For all we know, the citadel may have already fallen, in which case, Private Pollock, you will be on the mat in the morning."

"Seriously, Pollock," said Templeton, "we can't worry about things like that. In any case, I think that all these people are going to get into pretty fair trouble, whatever happens."

Pollock jumped nimbly out of the trench and with the non-committal words, "Well, it's a bad show," he retired into the farmhouse, leaving behind him a silent and thoughtful pair of sentinels in the trench.

Gardiner was not sure whether he had not gone too far and he thought it best to say nothing more. His companion was deep in thought. For a long time they watched. Night fell and the last of the gulls had retired to bed. It was nearly midnight before the unmistakable sound of oars galvanized the watchers to alertness. Leaning forward from the trench they could see the dark shape of a rowing boat, and then came up the sound of the keel crunching on the sand. Two figures crossed the narrow white strip of beach and were lost in the dark shadows of the cliff. The watchers edged away down the trench until a slight curve provided them with cover from anyone advancing up the path.

After a couple of interminable minutes the silhouette of a man on hands and knees appeared at the top of the path and moved steadily up to the farmhouse door. A second figure followed close behind.

Everything was dark inside the farm. The windows were shuttered and there was not a sound. The place might have been deserted. The crouching spies listened, with their ears to the shutter of the big room, just as Templeton had listened when he first ascended the path. Then they crept to the other window facing the sea and listened there, but again there was no sound.

For a minute the two men in the trench lost sight of the intruders in the shadow of the building. Templeton thought for a moment that they had slipped away unnoticed, but Gardiner, guessing from some tiny movement that Templeton had lost sight of them, laid a restraining hand on his knee. The next moment the two figures crept round the corner of the farm and began to make a slow circuit of the walls of the barn, inside the barbed wire defences.

Templeton whispered to Gardiner, "I can't see anyone down at the boat. I think these are the only two."

Gardiner leant over and stared into the darkness below. Finally he nodded. "I can't see anyone," he whispered back. Templeton made a trumpet of his hands and breathed into Gardiner's ear, "If they're suspicious we must stop them. If they find nothing, let them go." His companion nodded.

At least five minutes elapsed before the circuit was completed and the two men came crawling round the other side of the farm. They crouched at the top of the path for a moment and then with one accord straightened themselves up, and one spoke a short sentence in some foreign language. The other nodded and shrugged his shoulders and turned down the path; another moment and they would have been out of earshot, but just at that instant the unmistakable sound of a yawn came from one of the rooms of the farm and Griffin's voice saying, "Damn it, I'm tired. Bedtime."

At the first sound of the yawn Templeton had gripped Gardiner by the arm; before the sentence was half finished they had scrambled out of the trench and were barring with levelled pistols the path down the cliff. The spies had waited to hear the end of the sentence and that made them a fraction of a second too late. Dark though it was, they could see the outline of the pistols in front of them, and without hesitation or waiting to be asked they put up their hands. Templeton raised his voice a little and said, "Griffin, are you there?"

The door was unbolted and Griffin peered out. "Hullo, what is it?" he said.

"Prisoners of war."

"Ho, ho!" he replied. "Bring them in. So the great campaign has opened."

"What made you yawn like that? It gave the show away," said Templeton.

"Sorry," said Griffin, without much conviction in his voice. "I always forget these rules about keeping quiet after dark. I'll go and get the Chief."

The two prisoners, on being ushered into the dining-room, seemed rather dazed by the sudden reversal of fortune and the glare of the lights which Griffin had snapped on. Both were heavily armed and looked venomously at Gardiner as he politely removed pistols from their bulging pockets. They firmly refused to answer any questions put to them. Not even the violent threats which the old man thundered at them would make them divulge their names or their employers or any details of any plans against the farm. They simply relapsed into sullen silence.

Pollock, attracted from his watch by the animated conversation and the roaring sentences of the old man, came down and inspected the captures. "Hullo," he said. "It's your old friend, George, with the patent leather shoes. That was a bad blunder, my friend," he added severely. "Postmen don't wear patent leather shoes." It was the only remark that penetrated the silence of the prisoners. The man whom he addressed looked extremely disgusted and said sorrowfully, in excellent English, "Yes, that was a blunder," but not another word would he say.

De la Rey grew so violent in his rage and fury at their silence that he began to threaten the most terrific tortures, and even went so far as to send for his two laboratory men to help him. Templeton turned on him and said firmly, "We can't have any of that sort of thing."

The old man began to bluster, but Templeton interrupted him ruthlessly. "These are my prisoners — not yours. Another word and there'll be trouble." He insisted on locking the two men into one of the upstairs attics, after first making certain that the iron shutters were securely fastened.

"A neat bit of work," observed the Oyster dreamily, "for which I think I deserve the warmest congratulations. Don't thank me," he added. "It was easy for me. I don't suppose there'll be anything more tonight."

They had strolled out to the trench. After the dazzle of the electric light they found it difficult at first to focus their eyes on the darkness. Gardiner was the first to get accustomed to the change. He looked down at the beach below and was for the first time startled out of his usual equanimity. "Damn it," he exclaimed sharply. "There were three of them after all."

"What do you mean?" asked Templeton quickly.

"The boat has gone."

They leant over and could see that there was no longer the dark shape of a boat lying silhouetted against the sand.

"Yes," said Templeton soberly, "there'll be trouble now, and no mistake. But I doubt if anything will happen tonight. We had better go and get a good night's rest; I fancy tomorrow may be pretty busy. One sentry will be enough. He can walk round and round. I'll take the first shift."

CHAPTER XVII

The Attack

The day dawned hot and stuffy. There was no breeze, hardly even the faintest movement of air over the sea. The sky was cloudless and the sun blazed down incessantly. It was more like a day in the South of Europe than in the North of Scotland.

The little garrison assembled for breakfast in a grave and sober mood. The news that there had been a third spy on the previous night who had escaped, had brought home to them all the gravity of their position. Even the old man seemed to have lost a good deal of his optimism and he no longer talked of the impending change in the affairs of the world. He seemed to be harassed and nervous and he scowled perpetually at his plate.

The only person at breakfast who had any semblance of cheerfulness was the irrepressible Gardiner who chattered away to himself, to the girl, or to anyone who would listen to him. Templeton's only contribution to the talk was the sudden question, "Why not send for the police?"

The old man shook his head. "We are beyond the help of the police now, sir; they can't help us. In any case, I can't afford to call them in. Too many things have been done in the past. No, we must just go our own way."

Griffin was even more sardonic than usual. The girl, on the other hand, was as calm and cool as if she had been sitting down to breakfast in a country house before a day's golf or fishing. Pollock's behaviour was strictly correct and studiously polite. He kept on jumping up to pass the toast and to clear away plates, and each time drew from Griffin an irritating grin. Altogether it was a depressing meal and the hours that followed were even more depressing.

There was nothing to do except to wait. They passed a little time in laying two or three strands of barbed wire in the long grass some yards below the trench, but when that was completed there was nothing more to do. They had all finished the illustrated papers and the only books in the house were a couple of scientific treatises belonging to Griffin. They tried bridge but found it difficult to keep their attention on the cards.

At intervals De la Rey came out of the door and stared across the sea. He looked so worried that no one liked to speak to him. Templeton could not help wondering whether he was looking for help or whether he was wishing himself back in the scenes of his wild youth in distant countries.

An occasional diversion was the sight of a trawler or a small cargo boat passing along the coast. Gardiner tried throwing bread to the gulls but found that as a sport it quickly palled. His offer to play anyone at shove halfpenny met with no response.

Lunch consisted of bread and cheese, and was an even gloomier meal than breakfast had been. And so the hours dragged on, until at eight o'clock they assembled once more for supper. Griffin had unearthed a couple of bottles of champagne and attempted to give an air of gaiety to the proceedings. He filled up the glasses and said, "I'll give you a toast — to our next meeting." He drained off his glass and fell to on the cold tongue before him.

They were half-way through dinner when there came a crash on the slate roof, followed by a loud rattle and the sound of something falling outside. Gardiner was taking the watch, and as they tumbled out of the door, pistols in hand, they heard his voice shouting cheerily from above, "It's all right — only a stone. A man threw it from the road."

They found the stone lying between the farm and the sea. It had pitched on the slate roof and had dislodged a couple of slates. A dirty piece of paper was tied round it. Templeton undid it and read aloud: "Surrender and all lives will be spared except the Chief's. You have no chance against us. We give you one hour."

Griffin glanced at his watch. "That's until nine o'clock. It will still be light then. Surely they won't attack us in the daylight."

"You never can tell," said Templeton. "We had better start getting ready."

Pollock went up and relieved Gardiner for the latter to have some food, and then they distributed their forces. It was agreed that the most powerful attack was likely to come from the sea, partly because the wire entanglement on the land side was so strong, and partly because in a desperate law-breaking enterprise, such as a murderous attack upon a peaceful farmhouse, it would be much easier to advance and retreat by sea under cover of darkness, rather than to risk running the gauntlet of the police on land.

The garrison was paraded, therefore, and Pollock, with the silent laboratory assistant whose name was Grew, were detailed to defend the landward side. The old man, Griffin, Templeton, Gardiner, and Bevan, the second laboratory assistant, manned the trench. The girl was to remain inside the farmhouse and act as go-between to summon reinforcements to any part of the defence that was in need. She accepted her part as if she was accepting a cup of tea at the Carlton. It took about five minutes to make those arrangements and then the garrison found themselves with the best part of an hour on their hands.

The time seemed to pass even more slowly than during the day. The sun was beginning to sink, and the sea and the land were covered with long shadows. Griffin was standing at his post in the trench with a watch laid in front of him. "Ten minutes longer," he said, and then "Eight minutes," and then "Six minutes." At five minutes to nine there was a loud shout from the other side of the farm. Griffin turned and called over his shoulder, "What is it?" The girl opened one of the steel shutters an inch or two and called back, "A man got up on the dyke beyond the field and shouted 'Five minutes more' through a megaphone."

"Two minutes," said Griffin. "One minute." He picked up his watch, looked at it and quietly said, "Time." He put the watch in his pocket and picked up his pistol.

From somewhere across the fields came a loud, metallic sound, as if someone was beating a gong. It was struck nine times.

"Nine o'clock," murmured Gardiner. "How thoughtful of them."

They stared down at the cove below. Everything was quiet. The gulls had gone to bed. There was not a breath of air. The smoke of distant steamers was rising straight up in perpendicular columns. Far away across the smooth sea a three-masted sailing ship with red sails was becalmed. "Come on, boys, come on," said Gardiner, half to himself. "This is slow."

They could hear a motor passing along the road behind them, and the sound getting gradually fainter. Then there was the sound of a motor nearer at hand, then a single shot from the upper storey where Pollock was on guard, followed by a tremendous explosion. Everybody jumped; their nerves were on edge with the long waiting. A thousand gulls started from the rocks, wheeling and crying.

"What the devil was that?" said Templeton over his shoulder to Gardiner. The other shook his head. There was not another sound and the gulls gradually returned to bed. Griffin jumped out of the trench and ran into the farm. He re-emerged in a moment and jumped back into his place. "First blood to us," he said with a laugh. "They started up a Ford car and sent it empty against the wire-a sort of amateur tank. Pollock put a shot through the petrol and it blew up before it got to the wire. Pretty good nerve he must have."

"Good for Charles," said Gardiner. "I believe now he used to win revolver competitions in the Army, but still, to hit a petrol tank in one shot isn't bad."

The sudden and unexpected destruction of their improvised battering ram seemed to have disconcerted the attackers, for there was a long interval. "That seemed to give them something to think about," said Griffin. "I thought they would find the barbed wire a bit of a snag." He took a flask out of his pocket, took a good pull and passed it along.

The sun had set and twilight was coming on fast when Templeton suddenly leant forward and said, "Here they come." He had a dry feeling in his mouth which reminded him irresistibly of certain moments of the war. Three large rowing boats came pulling rapidly round the headland and made a dash for the beach. The moment their bows had touched the sand, the crews came tumbling ashore and, forming as if by magic into one long line, began a steady ascent of the slope.

Templeton glanced round at his companions and then at his spare cartridge clips and reserve pistol to see that they were in place. He rubbed his hands on his handkerchief carefully, to ensure a good, firm grip; then he looked at the steady advance coming up the slope. "They've done this game before. Don't fire till I give the word," he called out. He stood up on the fire-step and shouted to the attackers, "Stop, or we'll fire." The reply was a spasmodic ripple of shots which made him jump down hastily and the ascent continued steadily.

Templeton counted five and then called out, "Let them have it now!" and he began firing Steadily at the on-comers. There was a great rattle and blaze of shots from the other defenders. The target was too easy even for a bad shot to miss, and the assault crumpled up instantly. A few of the attackers threw themselves on their faces and tried to take cover behind any ridge of earth available, while the others frankly bolted back to the shore and raced for protection among the rocks.

Templeton and Gardiner immediately stopped firing but Griffin and the other man had obviously lost their heads in the excitement and went on banging their pistols off at random. They only stopped when Gardiner went along the trench and shook them roughly by the shoulder.

One by one the survivors of the attack who were lying concealed half-way up the slope took their courage in their hands and retreated until they were all under cover among the rocks on one or other of the two headlands. Then came a fusillade of sniping. The deepening darkness made the flashes redder and brighter and each shot was echoed many times backwards and forwards from the cliffs. The thud of the bullets in the parapet of the trench and in the earth below was occasionally varied by the metallic clang of a bullet against the iron shutters of the farm.

Templeton went along the trench to see if anyone had been hit. He found the old man kneeling on the improvised fire-step with a look of quiet satisfaction on his face and his rifle in a most professional manner under his chin. One glance sufficed to show Templeton that he had used a rifle before. "I should keep your head down, sir, if I were you," he said warningly.

"That's all right," said the old man. "I was just having a go at these snipers," and he cracked off another shot. "Just like old times," he added, as a cry echoed up from the direction in which he had fired.

Griffin was very pale but managed to raise a shadow of his sarcastic smile. "Old-fashioned warfare," he said. "You wait till we get going with the germs. They will change all this."

The comparative silence was broken by a rattle of shots from the other side of the house and then a series of heavy explosions. Templeton raised his voice and shouted to the girl in the farm, "Are you all right there? Do you want help?" After a pause her clear voice came through one of the shuttered windows: "They've been trying to blow up the wire with bombs but we've got them well in hand. I'll let you know if we want help."

The sniping from the rocks died down almost entirely and there was another breathless wait for something to happen. Templeton and Gardiner peered over the trench and tried to make out in the gathering gloom what was happening below. There seemed to be the outline of another boat coming round the headland but they could not be certain. Then there was a tremendous blast of rifle fire from below which swept backwards and forwards along the parapet of the trench.

"There's a machine gun there," shouted Gardiner. "Can you hear it?" Templeton nodded. "This looks bad," he replied. "Keep your head down." He crept along the trench to Gardiner and the two old soldiers had a whispered consultation.

"It's just like the war," said Templeton. "They're firing at the parapet of the trench to make us keep our heads down while the attackers come up

145

underneath. The moment they stop firing we must be ready to jump up. I've got a whistle. I'll blow it when I think they're coming. Pass the word down."

"It's a nasty business," said Gardiner.

"You're right," said Templeton grimly. "Pass the word along to jump up when I whistle." He returned to his post and waited for the storm of bullets to stop as abruptly as it had started. He knew that all this time the attackers were creeping up the hill, and the moment the rifle bullets ceased, they would be ready to jump into the trench. It was, therefore, of the most vital importance to detect the exact second at which the bullets would cease. He knelt at the bottom of the trench, with a pistol in each hand and his whistle between his teeth, listening intently with an ear that had once been expert in such things.

The moment he had been waiting for arrived at last. The sound of the rifles and machine guns suddenly died away. Blowing his whistle, he sprang up. He was not an instant too soon. There was a loud guttural shout from just below and a confused mass of dark silhouetted figures came heaving up the hill towards him. Again the thought flashed through his mind that these men were trained soldiers, and not hired assassins or Continental murderers.

The blaze of revolver shots from the defenders swept the attack down the hill again. Those in front who were hit rolled heavily back on those behind, and in the twinkling of an eye the assault was over.

It was now too dark to see what was happening on the beach and further shooting was useless. The invincible Gardiner, however, sprang from the trench, ran to the farmhouse and returned with a couple of chairs which he hurled down the cliff and followed up with a fender and two or three large stones. The fender in particular made an appalling sound as it bumped and jumped and rattled down to the beach.

"I believe they're off," said Templeton, peering down. "I think they've had enough." He reloaded his pistols. "It may be a trick; we had better wait and see."

Complete silence had succeeded the terrific clatter of the shooting; the moon began to rise and in the first faint light they could distinctly see heavy rowing boats pulling out of the cove. "Don't pursue," cried the old man excitedly. "It may be a trick," and he opened fire with his rifle at the retreating boats. An instant more and the last of them was round the point and out of sight.

A cautious survey by Gardiner and Templeton proved that none of the attackers had remained behind in ambush, and that the evacuation was, so far as they could make out, complete. They therefore left Bevan on guard and returned to the farmhouse, feeling a remarkable mixture of pride and relief.

Pollock came down from his post and they compared notes. On the land side, he said, the attack had been a very faint-hearted affair. After the failure of the Ford there were one or two spasmodic attempts to climb the wire by throwing cloaks and blankets over it, and there had been a feeble effort to blow a hole in the entanglement with bombs. "They were such open targets," said Pollock, "that I really hardly liked to take aim. It was like a coconut shy at the local fair."

"It was done on our side," said Templeton, "all according to the book. Infantry attack under cover of artillery and so on. They were hot stuff."

The girl had provided cold supper and they fell to ravenously. "A pretty good evening's work," said Templeton at last. "Without a single casualty on our side."

"And to think," said Gardiner, "that this is the law-abiding country of Scotland. It seems hardly possible. I wonder what the neighbours will think of our midnight battle."

"Probably didn't hear it," growled Griffin. "There aren't any of them within three or four miles that I know of."

Next morning there was nothing but the twisted metal of the destroyed Ford, the small holes in the ground made by the bombs, and the bullet marks on the wall of the house to show that the incidents of the previous night had really taken place.

CHAPTER XVIII

The Arrival of the Navy

After breakfast Templeton, who had been thinking deeply, said, with the air of a man who has made up his mind, "I think we ought to try to get out of here as quick as possible."

"And give up your chances of being a saviour of humanity?" said Griffin.

"Well, I think we only beat them off last night by good luck, and I doubt if we can do it again."

"Why not?" thundered the old revolutionary. "God is on our side."

"Well, that's one way of putting it," said Gardiner, "but I had much sooner we had the police."

"I tell you," said the other, "I can't have police inquiry into my actions. I have done nothing I am ashamed of but I have done a great deal that they would not understand. The police is out of the question."

"I had much sooner be misunderstood by the police," murmured Gardiner, "than shot up by those gentry of last night."

"It's the same thing so far as I am concerned," said the old man grimly.

"Oh, is it as bad as that?" said the barrister politely. "I should be very glad to defend you if it ever came to the Old Bailey."

The only thanks he received for this offer was a heavy scowl.

"Well, what about it?" said Templeton. "Shall we clear out?"

The old man suddenly changed his tone. "Only two more days," he said. "Hold the place for two more days — that's all I ask. It may even be only one day, but two at the most. Gallant fellows like you could do it easily. You are all brave soldiers."

"Well, speaking as a brave soldier," said Templeton, "I see no chance whatever of holding this place for another twenty-four hours if we're attacked again. Believe me, last night was a pure fluke."

"You have held it once, why not again?" said the other urgently. "I don't believe it was a fluke."

The girl came in at that moment. "There are a couple of policemen in uniform outside," she said. "They are at the gate in the wire entanglement."

All eyes instinctively turned on the old man. He rose and said, calmly and with dignity, "You may do what you like. I give you full authority." He took up his overalls, mask and gloves, and walked firmly out of the room towards the barn.

"Infernally awkward," said Gardiner plaintively, "being put on one's honour like that. We can't give the old blighter up."

The girl looked at him freezingly.

"I can't help it," said Gardiner bluntly. "Even though he is your father, he's an old blighter." She tried to stare him down but he refused to be overawed.

Templeton turned to Griffin who was looking at him with amusement. "Shall we go and talk to them, Templeton?" he said.

"It might be a dodge," said Pollock warningly. "It might be these fellows dressed up."

"I know one of them by sight," said the girl. "I remember seeing him when we were up here last time."

They went to the gate and found two country policemen in an obvious state of mingled civility and perplexity. Griffin unlocked the gate in the fence and the senior of the two policemen began at once. "That's a funny fence, sir. It's thicker than when I saw it last."

"Yes," said Griffin airily. "We have had a good many poachers about."

"We've had some funny reports, sir," went on the policeman. "I hear there was a lot of shooting in these parts last night."

"That's right," said Griffin. "There was lots of shooting. We were out after gulls."

"Gulls!" said the second policeman. "I never heard of anyone shooting gulls up here before."

"That's quite likely, officer," was the reply, "but we've got to have gulls for our fish. You know we're experimenting with fish?

The second policeman scratched his head. "I've heard of having to have fish for gulls, but not gulls for fish."

"Oh, it's a well-known scientific fact," said Griffin.

"Well, that's most surprising," said the policeman. "The stories we heard made out that there was a regular battle here last night, with bombs and explosions and things."

"Oh, that must have been the Ford," said Griffin with a laugh. "It blew up last night — that's all that's left of it. That and the echoes from the cliffs; you get some pretty powerful echoes round these parts."

"That's true," said the first policeman. "Well, so long as everything is all right, that's all we care about."

"Oh, everything is all right," said Griffin. "Sorry you've had your walk for nothing. There will probably be some more shooting tonight, by the way," he said. "We've got a good deal more to do."

If the policemen expected to be asked in for a drink they were disappointed, for Griffin, having politely said good-bye, firmly closed and locked the gate in the fence. He could see that the policemen, while accepting the story he told them, nevertheless instinctively felt that there was something wrong. He walked thoughtfully back to the farm and said curtly, "They've gone." Then he said to Templeton, "I don't think we could leave the place even if we wanted to; did you see those men out in the field?"

"I saw one man," said Templeton.

"There was a whole circle of them, like a cordon of sentries. You'll probably see them all right from upstairs."

From Pollock's observation post they could see distinctly half-a-dozen men posted at regular intervals guarding the approaches to the farm from the land.

"They've probably got a boat waiting round the corner," said Griffin, "doing the same for that side. There's mighty little chance of your getting away."

Templeton took Gardiner aside and said to him in an undertone, "What about going for help in one of the aeroplanes?"

"I had a look at them early this morning," whispered Gardiner. "They've taken the petrol out."

Templeton started. "Who has?"

"I expect it's the old Organizer of Liberty. Just like the sort of monkey tricks he would be up to. You see, the old boy is in a tight hole, apparently. If we got the police they would hang him, and if we leave him these other chaps will get him. His only chance is for us to defend him until the steamer comes back and takes him off."

"It's a pretty low trick," said Templeton indignantly, but Gardiner only shrugged his shoulders. "He's in a desperate corner," he said, by way of extenuation.

The day dragged on without incident. There was no attempt made either to launch a regular attack on the farm or to do any spasmodic sniping. The investing forces lay very low, with the exception of their ring of sentinels. At intervals the old man came out of the farm and swept the horizon with a pair of field glasses. As the afternoon wore on his appearances became more frequent, and at each disappointment his face appeared a little more haggard and a little more worried.

At about five o'clock Pollock reported the rather singular fact that the sentries had vanished. Gardiner volunteered to make an expedition to verify this, but Templeton refused to let him take the risk. They came down from Pollock's room to find the old man standing once again with the field glasses to his eyes, but instead of sweeping the horizon they were focused on a small boat that was making its way slowly along the coast at a distance of about a mile. Templeton glanced at it idly and then said, "That's not the ship you're looking for, is it?" He got no answer and the old man turned to the farm and shouted for Griffin. When Griffin came out he also took a long look at the strange ship without speaking, then he said, "It looks infernally like it."

"What looks most infernally like what?" said Templeton. "Friends of yours? If so, they're welcome. Good Heavens, man, what's the matter?" he went on, for Griffin, who had been pale during the battle, was now as white as a sheet. "That's a gunboat," he stammered.

"That's right," said Templeton. "They have lots of them on this coast; fishery gunboats." "Look at her nationality," said Griffin. Templeton looked through the glass and easily recognized the crimson flag floating at the stern of the little ship. "It's a coincidence," he said. "A damn funny one," said Griffin shortly.

"They wouldn't dare to land official troops on the coast," said Templeton. "It's out of the question. These things aren't done nowadays. It would mean war."

"Not necessarily," said Griffin recovering his sangfroid. "Not a bit necessarily. The Government would merely apologize, say the captain of the ship was mad, hang him and the crew, pay a huge indemnity, and that would be the end of it."

"But what an incredible risk it would be," said Templeton.

"Oh, they're prepared to take risks," was the dry answer. "They're prepared to go to any lengths to stop our little cargoes."

"Well, I won't believe it till I see it," said Templeton. "A couple of hundred years ago, perhaps, but not now."

As he spoke there was a red flash from the hull of the small boat, a shriek and a roar overhead, and an explosion from the fields behind the farm. A small column of smoke rose slowly above the ship and a dull boom came ashore on the light breeze. For a moment pandemonium broke out. Gardiner and Templeton, with the instinct of long experience, hurled themselves into the trench The old man stood paralysed for a moment, and then made for the farm. Griffin ran round in small circles, waving his arms and bleating unintelligibly.

Pollock's face appeared at the upper window and he shouted, "Who did that?" then he saw the ship lying motionless off the shore and the small cloud of smoke above it and his face fell.

Before anyone had recovered from their surprise a second shell pitched in almost the same place.

The girl came slowly out of the farm. She was smoking a cigarette and with the utmost deliberation she blew three perfect smoke-rings and watched them circle upwards in the sunlit air.

"Come into the trench, Susan," shouted Templeton. She looked down at him. "Why?" she asked, as if she was humouring a child. For answer he jumped out, seized her by the wrist and dragged her into the trench. "I'm not afraid," she said.

"Perhaps you're not," he replied. "I am." The old man had recovered his nerve and was easily persuaded to shelter in the trench. Griffin collapsed on the fire-step and lay there trembling. A third shell struck the cliff a few yards below them and there was a great whirring of rock splinters and patter of descending dust and earth. They huddled in the far corner of the trench, as much as possible out of the line of fire. Then Pollock appeared racing out of the farm. He jumped in beside them and said, "We must go and dig a hole at the back. I can't watch the barbed wire from the top of that farm. At least I could, but I'm damned if I'm going to."

The next shell pitched right into the dining-room and after the crash of the explosion there came a cloud of yellow smoke eddying back through the window. Part of the table was thrown backwards almost into the trench and a tin of preserved meat hit Gardiner on the arm. "They're getting hotter," he said. "No supper tonight. Come on, Charles, before the next one arrives."

They ran across the line of fire round the farm, dived into one of the barns for spades, and dived out again before the next shell neatly cut off one of the chimneys and exploded beyond the house. Working with feverish haste and lying down abruptly as each shell arrived, they succeeded in digging a hole sufficiently deep to shelter one man in such a position as to be slightly out of the line of the shells, and at the same time commanding a view of the wire.

Templeton and Gardiner then repeated their previous dash back to the corner of the trench. The shooting went on regularly and with a fair amount of accuracy. In a quarter of an hour the farm had been practically knocked to pieces. Then came a rattle of revolver fire from the back, followed by a tremendous crash as a shell pitched on to the roof of one of the barns. In the interval between that shell and the next one, the huddled group in the trench could hear a loud shouting and a voice bawling out the same phrase over and over again.

"Here they come again," said Gardiner to Templeton, looking down and pointing to rowing boats which were pulling round the corner of the headland. "Now we're for it." The machine guns opened fire from below, in the same way as on the previous night, and compelled them to keep their heads down.

The boats grounded and once more the attack started up the hill. It was evidently being closely co-ordinated with the shelling, for as it began the shells ceased to hit the farmhouse, but were directed at the trench. There were clearly some sharp-eyed observers on the gunboat.

"We must get out of this," said Templeton, as a shell pitched on the parapet of the trench and covered them with earth. "It's getting too hot; we must go back into the farm."

One by one they crawled on hands and knees out of the trench and took cover behind the ruined walls. Then the shelling and the machine gun firing stopped and the next moment the attacking wave came over the crest of the hill and tumbled into the trench. The defenders opened a destructive fire from the ruins of the farm but the attackers combined the utmost bravery with the utmost persistence. Regardless of their losses, they poured over the crest into the trench. In the safety of the trench they reorganized and then began to rush at the farmhouse ruins. For a few moments the defenders kept them back and then they once more were forced to retreat into the ruins of the barns.

Templeton found Pollock beside him, kneeling behind a pile of bricks and shooting at anything he could see. "What's happened on your side?" Templeton found time to ask, and Pollock laughed. "A shell pitched in the laboratory," he said, "and started the germs drifting inland. I shouted out what was happening and the other side soon tumbled to it and bolted. The first of the germ war — got him!" he added viciously, shooting at a man who was climbing out of the trench. "That man Grew is done in."

One corner of the barn had caught fire and the flames were now beginning to mount. "Here's a jolly business," mumbled Gardiner, creeping up to them. He was holding his pistol in his teeth and trying to tie his handkerchief round his hand. "One more rush and I think we're done." But the final rush did not come. There was a distant whistle, followed by the sound of a man shouting and then more whistles much nearer. There was a heavy boom from the sea and the defenders instinctively ducked, but the shell never arrived. Instead, there was a hoarse shout from below the cliff and the next moment the attackers evacuated the farm and the trench and tumbled pell-mell back to their boats. From behind came the sound of running feet, shouting and crisp words of command. "What's up now?" said Templeton grimly. He had only one clip of cartridges left. Then a voice behind them said, "Well, here's a fine mess," and they turned round to see Inspector Fraser of the Inverness Police. Behind him there were scores of police in groups and on the main road beyond could be seen a row of lorries. A number of police had already begun to tackle the fire.

Gardiner was the first to rise to his feet and bow gracefully. "Inspector Fraser," he said, "I believe? Allow me to tell you, sir, that you are a welcome guest."

The inspector shook his head. "Well, I never saw such a sight," he said, and then he pointed out to sea, where two long grey destroyers were racing up towards the little gunboat. "It's lucky for you that Invergordon isn't so far away and that we still have a navy," he said. "Now, young gentlemen, I think you had better have a drink and tell me all about it."

CHAPTER XIX

The Organizer of Liberty

The inspector listened in silence to a brief outline of the recent happenings. He made no comment until the story was finished, and then he said, "Well, gentlemen, I think you have had a very narrow escape." He pulled his handkerchief out of his pocket and held it up; it hardly stirred in the faint breeze. "Lucky there's no wind to speak of," he said, "or those germs would be all over the countryside by now."

He turned to a sergeant who had been standing behind and gave rapid instructions for a cordon of police to surround the fields in which the fatal cloud of yellow dust had settled and prevent anyone from passing the cordon. Then he took out his notebook and scribbled a message on a page which he tore out and handed to an orderly. "Take this to the nearest telephone," he said, "as quick as you can, and put that message through to Aberdeen University. Make it a priority call and don't leave the telephone until you've got the message through."

Another sergeant stepped up briskly and said, "There seem to be three of them dead up here, and a dozen or more down on the beach."

The inspector turned to Templeton. "You'd better come and see if you can identify any of the bodies," he said. They went into the ruins and found that the assistant Grew and the two prisoners had been killed. Bevan had been severely wounded and both Griffin and Gardiner had been slightly hit. The farm itself presented an extraordinary spectacle. It had been built of solid granite and part of the walls were still standing. The slate roof and the rafters had been blown to splinters. The partitions dividing the rooms and the ceilings had been so completely crushed and disintegrated that it was not easy to recognize the rooms themselves. As usual the shells had played some odd tricks. The staircase stood intact and led up to an empty gaping void which had once been the first floor landing. In the kitchen everything had been destroyed except a cup of coffee which had been put down on the floor when the shelling began. Not a drop was spilt. Bevan's bowler hat was found lying on the floor of one of the barns without so much as a dent in it. The illustrated papers had been whisked away by a shell with the exception of a full-page photograph of Miss Gladys Cooper. The survivors stared at the scene of destruction.

"By the way, inspector," said Templeton, "how did you get here so providentially?" Fraser laughed. "I heard a story this morning about a lot of shooting being heard in these parts last night. I hadn't heard that you had come back, but as soon as the local policeman reported that he had interviewed Mr Griffin, I began to put two and two together. I was just starting from Inverness to have a look at the place when I heard that a foreign fishery gunboat had arrived unexpectedly. It seemed an odd coincidence, and when I found out the nationality of the boat I sent a telephone message through to the naval authorities at Invergordon and asked them to stand by in case of emergency."

"Did you really think that they would go so far as to shell the coast?" asked Pollock.

"No, I never thought they would go so far as that," said Fraser. "I thought it would be more likely to be an armed landing party."

"We seem to be very short of feminine society this evening," said a gentle voice behind them.

They turned to see Gardiner looking thoughtfully at the ruins.

"What do you mean?" Templeton began and then stopped. "By Jove, you're right," he went on. "I haven't seen the girl since the inspector arrived."

"Nor the Organizer of Liberty himself," put in Gardiner. "If you ask me, I think they've both done a bunk. He did suggest that he was not particularly anxious to meet the police. I mean, he hinted that if it was left to him, he'd just as soon not make your acquaintance, inspector."

"I don't see where they could have gone to," said Fraser. "We surrounded the place completely."

"Well, my experience of them," said Templeton, "is that they are remarkably elusive people." He stepped out of the ruins and stared round. The next moment the girl's figure rose from the far end of the trench. He walked across and saw that at the bottom was the body of the old man. The Organizer of Liberty had been shot through the head. He looked from the body to the girl; her face was very pale and completely impassive. She held out her hand and said, "Help me out." He helped her out of the trench and without another look behind her she walked across to the farm. He beckoned to Fraser and in an undertone said, "There he is — he must have been hit in the final rush. Now that I come to think of it, I don't remember seeing him after we left the trench and fell back into the house. It's probably not a bad solution of the whole thing."

Fraser went across and looked at the body and Templeton went back into the farm. He saw the girl standing motionless amid the ruins of one of the barns. He picked his way across the heaps of rubble and granite blocks and timber to where she was standing. She watched his approach silently.

"What are you going to do now?" he said. "Is there anything I can do to help you?" She made no answer and he went on, a little nervously. "There must be many things to wind up and I'm sure I could be of use. You will need money and a place to go to. Have you any ideas?"

"If I have, they are no concern of yours," she said at last. She spoke without hostility but simply stated a fact.

"I thought, perhaps," he said hesitatingly, "that we have been through some bad times together, and I would like . . ."

"We have certainly had some bad times," she interposed, "and I am grateful to you and your friends for what you have done, but that is all over now. You have brought us nothing but bad luck ever since the first time you interfered. The kindest thing you could do would be to go away."

"But how will you manage alone?" he persisted. "There will be all kinds of arrangements to make and details to be seen to. If you will only accept my help for a day or two . . ." A harsh laugh behind him made him spin round. An improvised bandage round Griffin's head made him look even more sardonic than usual. It added a sort of rakish air. He was leaning against a corner of the building which had survived the shelling.

"The Saviour of Humanity claiming his just reward," he said, in an unpleasant tone.

"Stop it, Griffin," said Templeton. "Haven't you any decency?"

"Not much," said Griffin, "but at least I don't start badgering a girl five minutes after her father has died, which is what you seem to be doing. The knight errantry business rather palls if you don't get anything out of it. Is that it? The Damsel in Distress idea, eh? If you remove the distress you expect to get the damsel?"

"If you want to know what I was doing," said Templeton hotly, "I was offering to help in any way I could."

"Exactly," said the other with a laugh. "That's just the public school way of putting it. You always were a most confounded prig, Templeton. As for the lady," he went on, raising his voice to drown Templeton's reply, "you need not worry about her. I am her guardian and I will do all that is necessary."

Templeton looked at him, trying hard to discover whether he was speaking seriously or not. Griffin seemed to guess his thoughts, for he laughed again and said, "I don't expect you believe me, and I don't much care whether you do or not: the point is that the lady doesn't want you, so you had better get back to your golf. It's a pity you ever left it."

The girl intervened. "What's the use of quarrelling? We certainly haven't time to waste. We've got to start again, Jack, haven't we, and that will take time. We shall have to build up from the very beginning. We've got no money, no laboratory, no assistants. Everything is gone. We shall have to start from the very beginning."

Griffin looked at her coolly. "You can count me out," he said, pulling a long black cigar out of his pocket as if it were a fountain pen, and looking at it in a detached manner. The girl took a step forward and then said in the ominously calm voice that Templeton had learnt to recognize. "How do you mean? Count you out?" She compressed her red lips so that her mouth seemed even smaller than usual.

Griffin put the cigar in his mouth; it gave him a still more rakish look. "I've had enough of this business," he said. "It's too damned dangerous. I don't mind running ordinary risks, but when it comes to battle, murder and sudden shelling on a large scale, then I quit."

"Do you mean to say that you're going to let us down?"

"I'm not letting anyone down," he replied. "I did my best for your father, and now it's all over you don't catch me starting again."

"It's not all over," she answered. "It's only half-way through. If you leave us now you'll be a traitor."

"Oh, tut, tut," he said. "What words to use."

"Why did you come into it at all?" she asked. "Why did you come and work for father? You couldn't have had much conviction if you are prepared to throw your hand in now."

"Conviction!" said Griffin with a terrific sneer. "Conviction? No! Do you think I believed in your father's tinpot schemes for revolutions and liberty and all that rubbish? I came into it to get you, and for no other reason. It was the only chance I had. When we met that time in California I should never have seen you again if I hadn't accepted your father's offer to help him. It looked like Providence that he should have wanted a chemist just at the time when I was looking for a job. Liberty? Fiddlesticks! But you are a different matter." He dropped his indolent pose against the wall and took a step forward. "Can't you see?" he said. "The whole game is up — finished — blown sky high. Look at all the people we started with. Where are they now? Your father is dead, Morton is dead, Grew is dead, Bevan is so badly hit that he will be dead in a few days, Alexandrovski is dead, and the Irishman who did the business for us over there — the whole lot of them are gone and the game is gone with them."

She stamped her foot. "It isn't gone," she exclaimed. "We must carry on. Don't you see all the more depends on us as we are the only survivors? We've got to do the work of twenty now."

Templeton felt as if he were in the audience in a theatre. The two actors paid not the slightest attention to his presence. "Don't you realize," she said, "that the contract has not been carried out? We haven't delivered the last part of the consignment. We must complete it."

Griffin had come down to earth again. "It can't be done in the time," he said. "It would take months before we started producing again. Anyway, they've got enough to make a start. The Captain will have taken that first load across by this time; that will have to do.

"As for not fulfilling that contract, no one could have done more than we have. I tell you straight, I'm through. Let's go back to California and start again. I could always get work there and we can chuck this business entirely."

"And you expect me to go to California with a rat?" she said with devastating scorn. "You think that I'll give up my father's work when his body is lying within a yard or two of us?"

Griffin shrugged his shoulders. "It gives me the creeps," he said callously, "when I think that it might have been mine. Sooner his than mine." He lit the cigar and leant back against the wall.

The girl turned slowly to Templeton and said, "Mr Templeton, a few minutes ago you offered to help me. I accept your offer gladly."

Griffin chuckled but said nothing. "I'm glad," said Templeton. "I'll do my best for you, but I must make it absolutely clear that I am not offering to help you to make any more germs or to start your work again, but I will escort you to any place you like and I'll see that everything is done that is necessary."

"That is all I ask," she said. "The honour of my father is my own affair, and I will look after it myself. I shall set to work again as soon as I can."

"Why not chuck it?" said Templeton, almost involuntarily.

"You don't understand," she replied. "There are thousands and thousands of people who are waiting for the final consignment that will enable them to start their fight for Liberty. They have made a contract with my father to supply them; they have given us their money; the contract is not yet finished. My father has never let them down. He never let anyone down. I shall never rest until I have supplied them. In the meantime, they will have to start with what they have got." Gardiner's voice echoed with painful distinctness through the ruin. "So that's the end of the jolly germs," he was saying. "Half of them in a north-country river and the other half waiting to be lassoed by Aberdeen professors."

"And a good job too," came the reply in Fraser's voice. They passed round the outside of the building.

"What does that mean?" said the girl.

"It means," said Templeton steadily, "exactly what he said. We threw the first half into a river in Cumberland on our way up here. The packing cases that went abroad had nothing in them but earth."

She looked at him and then said, "So we have let them down after all."

"It has saved the world," said Templeton, "from a hideous calamity."

She did not seem to hear. "I wonder what they will be thinking about my father now," she said. "They will probably be opening the boxes today. And he never let anyone down while he was alive."

Griffin removed his cigar and said, "Well, that's that."

The girl walked past them and out of the ruins. The two men instinctively followed. She went across to where the police officers had laid the body of the old man, looked at it for a moment, and then set out with firm strides away from the farm at Gulls' Cove.